[partly obscured]ucation

Nick McDonell was born in 1984 in New York City. A graduate of Harvard University, he is the author of two previous novels, *Twelve* and *The Third Brother*. *Twelve* has been adapted for film by Joel Schumacher.

Also by Nick McDonell

Twelve

The Third Brother

An Expensive Education

Nick McDonell

Atlantic Books
LONDON

First published in the United States of America in 2009
by Grove/Atlantic Inc.

First published in Great Britain in 2009 by Atlantic Books,
an imprint of Grove Atlantic Ltd.

This paperback edition published in Great Britain in 2010
by Atlantic Books.

This novel is entirely a work of fiction. The names, characters
and incidents portrayed in it are the work of the author's imagination.
Any resemblance to actual persons, living or dead, events or localities,
is entirely coincidental.

1 3 5 7 9 10 8 6 4 2

A CIP catalogue record for this book is available from
the British Library.

ISBN: 978 184887 063 5

Printed in Great Britain

Despite the use of some real names, this is a novel. I have distorted institutions, tribes, languages, and geographies.

Dedicated to THCM and in memory of GAP.

"Did you believe it?"

"Not all of it. They haven't left us much to believe, have they?—even disbelief. I can't believe in anything bigger than a home, or anything vaguer than a human being."

"Any human being?"

—Our Man in Havana
Graham Greene, 1958

PART I

Boston, Massachusetts, 200X

The large Victorian is dark and cool, silent in the autumn night. Professor Susan Lowell lets herself in and carefully closes the front door behind her. Upstairs to check on the children she catches her reflection in the mirror in the dark hall and almost nods to herself in the silence. She is frowning. Not even midnight and they are all asleep, daughter, son, even husband. She grows slowly angry with them for this, and lets the feeling wash over her and recede.

Downstairs she picks up the remote and finds a muted news channel on the wall-mounted television. Her hair is down but she is still in her suit and heels. She knows some of the players, and a smile turns the corners of her wide mouth when she sees her own image. She wonders if the pleasure she feels at this moment is finer than all the pleasures to come. She has won a Pulitzer Prize, and her husband doesn't know yet.

One thing at a time.

She walks to the kitchen, opens a bottle of red wine, and takes a delicate glass from the cupboard. Back in the living room, she lowers herself onto the cloth couch, watches the muted news, drinks. When the bottle is half empty she goes upstairs, strips, and has her husband inside of her before he is fully awake. She tells him about the prize after she comes, before he comes. They talk afterward, but not for long. And then, cooling and finally tired, before she drifts into sleep, she thinks, Why am I afraid?

1

Kenya-Somalia Border, 200X

That morning a young American named Michael Teak drove north through the rolling scrub on a mission for his government, which was at that time the most powerful in the world. A kite, hunting on well-traveled winds from the Indian Ocean, floated overhead as his Land Cruiser bumped slowly over the remote track. Teak was in no hurry to reach the village under the white sun of the afternoon. Evening would be cooler and, he hoped, calm.

It was a simple mission, really. Deliver some money and a cell phone to a rebel named Hatashil, take a look around. *Too good to be true* had been Teak's first thought when he finished reading the file on Hatashil. Hatashil was a freedom fighter. An autodidact orphan warrior. A humanitarian and a leader. Teak was trained to be wary of those words, as if promise too bright was never fulfilled, ultimately betrayed. *Daylight on colonial brick.*

But Teak had been comfortably in-country for a year and a half and also thought that maybe it didn't have to be that way.

Or at least he didn't have to be that way. He wasn't sure. This was his problem and as he drove deeper into the green and brown landscape he felt disconnected from his surroundings, and then alienated too from his car, his gun. It occurred to him that finally on the right kind of mission, he might be the wrong kind of guy. He chalked this up to nerves and drove on, which was what, he understood at age twenty-five, a professional did.

There were five suitcases in the backseat. Cheap luggage for poor travelers, inelegant, plastic. They were Teak's second cover. He stopped the truck and consulted his phone, checking his position against the village coordinates. On track, on time.

As he shifted back into gear, Teak noticed movement on the horizon. Through a gap in a stand of acacias far down the track, a dust cloud. It was the first dust he had seen in over a hundred miles and he resumed his drive at a faster pace. He lost sight of the cloud, caught sight again as it rose over the trees. At best a lunatic safari, at worst—Teak briefly recalled the tortures that had befallen to one of his predecessors, his jellies scooped out, his abdomen cut to bits on rusty blades. Tied to a tree and left to die. No reason to waste a bullet.

Three vehicles. They stopped, lined up across the track. Teak stopped too, a mile out, and looked at them through his monocular. A white minivan, of the sort that usually safaried Japanese tourists, and two rusted pickups. Teak watched the men riding in the back of the trucks jump out and pull a metal gate off the roof of the van. All armed.

Shifta, Teak thought, tensing. In Amharic the word meant *social bandits*. A whole story distilled into a single word. *Wrongdoer*. He drove toward them.

* * *

The *shifta,* twenty-two of them by Teak's count, waited for him. They were younger than he expected and rich, with the van and that gate, which they had set up across the track. *Might be a particularly shrewd crew,* Teak thought.

Two men stood directly in front of the gate. One wore camouflage pants and a T-shirt with the D.A.R.E. antidrug logo. The other wore mesh shorts and a khaki safari shirt. Both carried Kalashnikovs. The man in shorts also wore a leather shoulder holster.

"Hello," said Teak, sticking his head out the window as he slowed. Best to use English, *lingua idiota.*

"Checkpoint," said the man in the antidrug shirt.

Teak stopped and let the Land Cruiser idle. He looked off to the sides of the track. He could drive around them but then they might chase him, shoot at his tires, probably miss, but maybe break his windows. Maybe worse. *Better to talk.* A boy holding a cleaver sat cross-legged on the side of the track, staring at Teak. *Strange.* Usually no children with the *shifta.* Teak winked at the child but the child just stared.

"Checkpoint?" said Teak, in his best baffled colonial, "on whose authority?"

The two men in front looked at each other. Mesh Shorts theatrically drew an old .38 from his shoulder holster. "Authority of General Hatashil," he said, tapping the rear door of the car with his pistol. "What's here?"

"Shit," Teak said for their benefit, putting his head in his hands.

They opened the doors, pulled the suitcases out onto the dirt, and ripped one open.

"You know, there's a zipper on that you could use," said Teak.

A cheer went up when they saw that grey-green khat filled the case.

Teak shook his head.

"You have a problem?" asked the shoulder holster boss.

"No," said Teak, suddenly brightening and extending a hand out the window. "I'm Teak."

"I am Commander Moalana," said the man in mesh shorts, surprised, briefly taking Teak's hand in a kind of half shake. Teak smiled at him and Moalana began to stroke his chin. He was almost gleeful, toying with Teak for his men, extremely grateful that this lone man with his bags full of drugs had crossed his path.

Moalana's men had been frustrated that morning. But then, Moalana reflected, they're frustrated all the time. He could take the car, too, but orders were orders. Restraint, Hatashil had said. After they had killed that last man as a spy, Hatashil had been angry. "We do not leave our allies tied to trees!" Hatashil had calmed down quickly, though, and delivered a lecture. "Misunderstandings happen," he had concluded, "but always restrain yourself." Moalana had been grateful for Hatashil's understanding in the face of so great a blunder.

Moalana offered Teak a bit of khat. Teak accepted and began to chew. He did not enjoy the bitter taste, like cabbage. "Can I keep one?" he asked.

"One bag," Moalana laughed for the benefit of his men, "how will you keep one?"

Before Teak could answer, Moalana cut him off. "Not one," he said, and his men began loading the cases into the trucks. The boy sitting cross-legged, Teak noticed, had become distracted from robbery and was drawing in the dry dirt with his cleaver. An older boy called to him as the rest of the *shifta* put the gate back on top of the van and lashed it in place.

Moalana waved his hand once from the window of his truck as it passed.

Teak spat the khat out and watched them disappear down the track. The whole encounter had taken less than five minutes. The khat cases had worked. He was still in no hurry.

Miles down, hours later, off a track off the track, the scrub dissipated into rocky plain, but first, a blessed stream. On the bank a crooked date palm, a dozen huts, goats, and naked children like miniature guardian angels. Teak liked the look of it. He parked a hundred yards from the village so as not to further disturb the corraled livestock. A few tattered goats bleated at the Land Cruiser.

From his pocket, a key, and Teak unlocked the glove box, took out a sealed FedEx envelope. He stepped out of the car and stretched his legs, reflecting on the temperature as he put on the wrinkled jacket of his khaki suit. He wore the same thing everywhere, and it was cooler now. Not that he minded the heat. His pale skin had a permanent burn but that was fine with him. A short lifetime of New England winters had been enough. He checked the SIG P220 in his waistband, tucked the FedEx envelope under his arm, and walked to meet the children approaching him through the dry crackle of the burnt grass. Behind them, leaning mothers, knowing disdain.

Then the most curious of the children was at his knee, looking up at him. Teak greeted the child in the local dialect, and the child was not old enough to find this strange.

"Riddle!" said Teak, grinning whiter teeth than the child had ever seen in a grown-up.

"Riddle me!" said the child.

"My house has no doors," said Teak. It was an easy and famous riddle about an egg, but the child was so young that Teak guessed it could be new to him, and he was right. The child ran back to commiserate with his fellows.

As Teak entered the village everyone stared. Two teenage boys waved antique Enfield rifles at him. One asked Teak his business, in English.

"Come to see Hatashil," said Teak cheerfully, surprising them with their own language.

The boys looked at each other and pretended to consider the situation. Puffing up, they told Teak to follow. They walked down to the stream. Under the date palm three men sat on a thick but worn rug, sipping from small bowls of fermented camel milk. Two in full camouflage, one, whom Teak immediately picked for Hatashil, in a white djellaba. They rose when Teak approached. Hatashil, also the shortest of the three, was heavy-set, almost fat. He was also vaguely lighter skinned, Teak noted, and had sharper features. He carried a walking stick topped with some kind of skull, Teak couldn't tell what species. He looked at Teak with heavy, recessed eyes and dismissed his associates, who walked down the stream with the two rifle boys. When they were beyond hearing, Hatashil gestured Teak to the rug.

They exchanged greetings and sat down. Teak complimented Hatashil on the rifle boys' English capabilities.

"If only mine were better," responded Hatashil, "but thank you. They are good boys. At the camp, we have even better."

A smiling, grasshopper-thin woman brought a tray of dates, goat cheese, and two cans of Fanta. *Cans instead of bottles,* thought Teak. *That's new.* Bowing, the woman put the tray on the rug between Teak and Hatashil. Hatashil smiled at her and she might have blushed.

Out of politeness, Teak ate a piece of the cheese. After that, neither man touched the food. Hatashil described to him the number of men, weapons, horses, and vehicles he had in a nearby camp. He pointed across the stream to where his own truck was parked. It was a Toyota pickup with a 12.7 millimeter machine gun mounted in the bed.

Teak opened the FedEx envelope with a folding knife and passed it across the tray to Hatashil. Hatashil looked inside and saw, to his satisfaction, many American dollars.

"Twenty-five thousand," said Teak. Then he reached into his pocket for a black cell phone, which he also handed over.

"Will I be talking with you?" asked Hatashil.

"No. You'll be talking with my colleague."

"It is too bad to make agreements with men who might be good men and then never to see them again," said Hatashil, sliding the phone open and turning it on.

Beep.

High above them, in one of the random afternoon cumulus formations, an alarm went off and a pilot adjusted his course.

Teak heard the slow drone of an Antonov as he was walking back to his Land Cruiser. He should have noticed it approaching from farther off, but he hadn't. *Aerial ordinance*. And then he was concussed forward through the air onto his face. Dazed, he rolled as a wave of heat blew over him. The date palm was splintered. The wooden corral was gone, only a crater left behind. The air was thick with dust. Belly-down in the dirt, Teak saw Hatashil's truck speeding away from the stream. He forced himself to his feet and ran to the Land Cruiser, where he retrieved the first aid kit from under the backseat. Teak was all training. He didn't look at the dead as he ran back into the village; he looked for the almost dead. The spot fires repeated the heat of the midday sun in the dusk.

He heard the grind of Humvees arriving from the east and saw a chalk of paramilitaries bearing down on what was left of the village. One of the Enfield boys ran toward the Humvees and they shot him down. The other had run in the opposite direction and one of the Humvees was chasing him.

Teak ducked into one of the charred huts. The woman who had brought him the cheese and Fanta lay facedown. A trail of blood led from the door to the thin pallet where the woman had dragged herself. An adolescent girl sat next to her, rubbing at her own ears, trying to restore her hearing. Teak knelt down beside them. Turning the woman over he saw, in the shiny gash across her neck, that it was too late for her.

He was reaching for the girl when he noticed at his feet a mug, the sort that he had received in his alumni package when he had graduated from college four years before. It was crimson, with the Harvard shield on it and, in white letters, the word *Veritas*. Teak did not have time to think about this before he heard the crack of M4s and felt the whistle of a bullet through the hut. Teak threw himself over the girl.

2

Jane had been in Deadalus a million times but never at this time of day. She couldn't remember the last time she had been up this early. All the volunteering at the homeless shelter was in the afternoon, and so were all the political round tables about abortion and the fate of the African Union and so on, and meetings at the *Crimson,* the school newspaper. And she drank, of course, prided herself on it. So she was never up before eleven. Sometimes she drank scotch, because that's what those boys at the Kennedy School of Government drank, but she liked screwdrivers better.

She sat with David at the empty bar. They ordered salmon eggs Benedict, a weekly treat for him. She coffee and bloody mary, he only orange juice. Sometimes, when they were out, she wanted him to drink more because he didn't drink, at least not like the rest of them. But he made up for it. He was six-four, almost six-five in the four-hundred-dollar Prada boots she had given him for his birthday. And black. And she was so white and blonde. And she said it was *no thang,* ha ha, when they had started dating. He never brought it up. Last night she had been out with her girlfriends.

"Thanks for getting up," said David. He was always thanking her for things. His voice had the low drip of British colonial schools. It drives me wild, Jane told her mother.

"Such a geek," she laughed. "Glad you can fuck."

David, even after seven months, didn't know how to respond when she said things like that. But he liked it.

She ran her hand over his back. He wore thrift-store shirts. This one, thin and yellow, had someone else's monogram on the pocket.

"So, why are we up so early?" she asked.

David pulled an envelope out of his backpack. She liked the shirt but wished she could just buy him a good bag, like the leather Varvatos satchel her mother had bought her father. David had this Eastpak backpack that he had brought with him from home. He handed her the envelope. The paper was heavy and cream colored. His name was handwritten in black ink. On the back, a red wax seal had been broken. The seal had been the head of a pig.

"This came under my door last night."

"The Porcellian punched you," said Jane as soon as she saw the broken seal. She grabbed the card. Another pig face was embossed on the paper, in green. Handwritten again: *The President and Members of the Porcellian Club request your presence for cocktails at* . . . the invitation continued with the address of a building just off campus. Eight o'clock, the next Tuesday.

"Hilarious," said Jane, slapping the heavy invitation on the bar.

"Here, be careful," David reached for it.

"You're actually thinking about doing this?" Jane held the card away from him.

"Try it all, once," he said. She had said that to him many times.

"Yeah, but not this. This is the worst, paternalist, classist, homophobic, old boy bullshit." *This was her boyfriend, damn it, not a final-club boy.* She took a breath, "God, I sound like a sociology grad student. But really, David."

"I don't have to join just because I go."

"They're just glorified frats. You don't need this bullshit. You've got enough steam on your own. Don't they have any idea where you're from? Most of the boardroom assholes who engineered your country onto page twenty-six of the *Economist* were probably in the Porc. What do you think Hatashil would say about that fucking club?"

"I think you shouldn't swear so much," said David quietly, self-righteously. "I also think my country is more complicated than that. And how am I to know what Hatashil would say? He says that we should educate ourselves."

"Forget the world, just on campus they're assholes." Jane could not stop talking. Her bangles jangled as she reached down near the hem of her flowery skirt and picked up her vintage purse. She took out a Moleskine notebook, ripped out a page, and drew a diagram as she went on.

"So, okay, there's the Porc, the most secret, secret blue-bloody weirdness. Make you jack off into Geronimo's skull like Skull and Bones. Or you could join the Fly and pop your collar and blow coke like you have to swim to Gatsby's green light. Or you could pop your collar with the A.D. and play lacrosse and funnel beer till you vomit all over the working class. Or the Phoenix. They have some black people, princes of Nigeria and like that. Maybe the Spee? They even have a Jew or two."

"Jane—" David interrupted. But Jane was riffing now, cracking herself up.

"Or, why join a final club? If you want to self segregate you might as well join the Asian American a cappella club, or some other wing of the silent majority. You work all the time anyway, you could just disappear into ballroom dancing and stop drinking entirely, like the half of people we never see here. Or laugh when you fart and become a *real* alcoholic and disappear into the *Lampoon* and never leave the castle? Maybe play football? You've got the body for it. But then I suppose they're all in the Delphic, Owl, or Fox. Can't have one without the others."

Jane took a breath and a long suck from her seven-dollar Bloody Mary.

"Wasn't your father in a final club?" David looked at the incomprehensible mess of lines and boxes on Jane's sheet of paper.

"Yes, he was." Jane sighed. "The Porc." She took her drawing back. "Look, babe, you're just too good for all that stuff. Look what you've done already. You walked out of the desert."

David found this patronizing. It wasn't desert, it was scrub. And he hadn't walked the whole way but she always liked to say it like it was some great trek. Especially around other people. He had just walked part way to town, once, from his cousins' village. People did it, if they didn't have a car or a camel or a horse. It was a long road, but the *shifta* didn't bother you if you had nothing for them to steal. Or at least, that's how it was when he was a boy.

But David said nothing. He liked being her hero and the story seemed to make her happy. He knew it must seem almost supernatural to her. And his heart warmed when she called him babe. It was so sunny and sexy and strange, so American. Once, in Annenberg, the freshman dining hall, waiting for a chickwich, he had heard another girl talking about Jane. She had called Jane a Beacon Hill bohemian. The girl hadn't said it nicely, but David thought it sounded pretty good.

"Several American presidents were members of the Porcellian," said David. He knew this would set her off.

"They're criminals. The CIA came out of Skull and Bones and *there*. Are they idols of yours, too? And half of that stuff is probably myth anyway. It's all just flip-cup played on mahogany."

They ate their eggs and salmon. "You know what," Jane said finally, "do what you want to do. Why not? They have events where you bring a date. Make the first cut and I'll come to the one where you need a date and we'll have a few drinks. Or at least I will."

"I would just like to get as much as I can out of this place. I mean," David felt foolish as he said it, "it *is* Harvard."

"Harvard is bullshit," she said.

3

That same morning on the other side of campus, Professor Susan Lowell found her office full of roses. In vases precariously balanced on her crowded shelves, in bouquets high on cabinets, on the stacks of books around her desk. Like the other offices in the Knafel building, hers was decorated in matte metal and tan wood. Light poured through her window, which looked out to the gray Gothic spire of Annenberg, where the freshman stumbled in to their breakfast. The roses—red, yellow, white—struck her as both well-illuminated and alien. Which was, more or less, how she was feeling that morning. The day before, she had won the Pulitzer.

The prizes had been delayed that year, so there was even more attention on them than usual. She had been stopped and congratulated four times on her way to the office. Now, she closed the door behind her and slumped into her Aeron chair. Before she could clear the roses from her desk and pull up the *New York Times* on her laptop there was a knock at the door. She told whomever it was to come in but did not look up, busying her hands with the roses. It was her habit to always be doing something else while she took meetings with students, especially the young men who arrived first thing in the morning and tried to make soulful academic eye contact. Not that she wasn't paying attention.

"I had a long celebration in your honor last night."

Susan's head snapped up at the flat, British voice. She knew those cadences. An old friend, Razi Farmian, stood just inside the door. A day of stubble shadowed Razi's pointed jaw, and the dark-skinned Iranian wore a rumpled tweed suit. *Finally,* she thought, someone she wanted to congratulate her. She came around the desk and then leaned down to hug him. She was nearly six feet tall, he five-seven. He smelled of gin and yesterday's Marlboro Reds. She of Jean Louis Scherrer perfume.

"You smell rich," Razi said. She was famous among the students for her chic suits, height, and waspy blonde good looks. And the Chanel sunglasses, and for being a hard-ass. She was thirty-six.

"Where did you sleep?" she asked, looking at her old friend's battered leather briefcase. She remembered him carrying it around the Ogaden, even. Sometimes there was nothing in it but a clean shirt.

"Wherever," he said, clearing roses from a chair and sitting down. "I'm sober, and I have three pieces of information."

Susan's BlackBerry buzzed. It was her husband, Harry, with annoying news. Their nanny, Sheila, was in New York, *remember?* and the deal he was working on was stretching out, so it would be hard for him to pick up the kids. Susan rubbed her eyes and agreed to deal with it. Either she would ask another mother to take the kids for a play date or she would pick them up herself. She hung up and looked at Razi.

"First," said Razi, ticking off a finger, "President Randolph is going to announce a cocktail party in honor of the two faculty Pulitzer winners."

"That's customary."

"Second, my fellowship is being jeopardized by a gray-eyed sophomore who wants me to fuck her like a goat. Do you think there's a rule against Nieman Fellows and undergraduates?"

"Ha ha."

There was another knock on the door, but before Susan could answer, Professor Henry Rose leaned in. Chair of the history department, Rose was immaculate in his three-piece pinstripe suit with pocket silk. Perhaps the reason he and Susan had always gotten along was their mutual appreciation of good clothes. It certainly wasn't politics. He had been a special foreign policy advisor to the Reagan administration and was a cofounder of a small but powerful think tank embraced by the so-called New Right. Rose raised his well-trimmed white eyebrows when he saw Razi, whom he knew both as a journalist and one of the Shah's many cousins.

"Excuse me," Rose said, "I didn't realize you were in a meeting."

Susan looked at him without smiling as he congratulated her and explained that President Randolph would be hosting a cocktail party in her honor and also in the honor of Tudo Denman, the English professor whose novel had won a Pulitzer. "Just wanted to let you know before the deluge," he said, nodding at the hallway. "A gathering storm of respect." He nodded to Razi and then turned out the door on his bench-made heel.

Susan followed him out into the hallway where she found four undergraduates, students in her lecture course, hoping to drop in. They all said congratulations at once. She thanked them for understanding how swamped she was, especially now, and told them to please e-mail for an appointment or come by during office hours on Monday. She closed the door not quite in their faces and turned back to Razi, who was toying with one of the roses.

"So, what's your last piece of news?"

"It has to do with your prize-winning account, I'm afraid," he said, putting the rose down. His voice went flat. "A couple days ago I ran into sainted humanitarian Roger Knustle, propping up the bar at the Cellar. He's back and told me that you, since the book, are still very much persona non grata."

"What's he doing back here?"

"A Carr Fellowship and a book about the U.S. Special Forces in the Horn. Good story that everyone knows, hasn't been done yet, and so on."

"He is such an asshole."

"He blows hard. But once we got through all the chalk talk—Delta is 'really tearing it up on the dance floor in Addis' —he told me that Hatashil's people are coming apart, murdering each other. The 'new' position is that Hatashil's movement was no such thing and would be over by Christmas. Apparently Hatashil forgot to tell us he's a lost Saudi royal nephew."

"That's bullshit," Susan said, but this was something she had never heard and it worried her.

"Of course, you're the only one who's ever met him," Razi said, picking up the rose again. "Anyway, you're right, Roger's an asshole. But then, yesterday, I put in a call to tell Toma about your prize."

Toma Ali Mugabo was their fixer in East Africa. It was rare that a fixer would operate in several countries but as they always said, Toma was singular. He was a Rwandan national who sometimes spoke in vintage rock-and-roll lyrics. Sometimes they had found this amusing, and sometimes not. Toma had introduced Razi and Susan in a bar in the Westlands section of Nairobi when Razi was a correspondent for *Time* and she was researching the dissertation that would become her book. Toma had seen the potential in connecting them.

"Come on down, sweet Virginia," Toma had said, sweeping his hand toward the bar where Razi was sitting, "a friend to help you through." Razi had stood up, surprised at how pretty Susan was. He liked the lyrics that time. Then Toma had bought them a round of Tuskers and told them to *drop their reds, drop their greens and blues*.

Once, in dry Khartoum after they had been interviewing UN officials for two weeks, Toma had brought them up an alley staircase to the back door of an Ethiopian restaurant. The sign on the door read *Infidels Bar*. A bouncer in a fez at a card table had them sign papers acknowledging that their souls were lost forever and releasing the proprietors and state from liability. Toma left them at the door. Inside, they drank Dewar's and toasted Toma's health. Ultimately, Toma had arranged Susan's introduction to Hatashil.

"'Positively Fourth Street,'" said Susan. "I have to call him."

"He was very happy for you. He also said that a whole village of Hatashil's wives and their children had been killed and no one knows who did it. Thirty people, half related to Hatashil. Latest epilogue to your epilogue."

Pause. Razi shifted tone.

"I can pick up Emily and Ford," he said. He was Emily's godfather. "I don't have anything to do this afternoon."

Susan told him that would be great and what to do. They made a plan for lunch later in the week and Razi left. Susan stared out the window. She'd met some of Hatashil's wives. She wondered which were dead. As horrified as she was at the news, a part of her was relieved. Now she had something to work on. But then, for the first time in as long as she could recall, her work felt vulgar. *Again,* she thought, *work to do*. She opened the contacts on her laptop but continued to stare out the window.

4

Teak sat on the hood of his Land Cruiser and watched the diminishing smoke curl into the cooling pink sky. He wanted to be visible. He had turned the girl over to a soldier who told him not to go anywhere, and had been sitting there for close to an hour, waiting to see how they would approach him. Teak recalled the first time he had been in Africa. On safari. It had all been about the animals then.

The paramilitaries were spread out around the village, smoking. One of them walked toward Teak. A medic, Teak could see from his kit. It was about time, but then maybe it wasn't. The dropping sun cast the medic's shadow long and strange, gun and gear projecting Gothic silhouettes over the broken ground. Behind him, the Humvees were parked in a star formation around what was left of the village. The two surviving villagers sat under guard.

"My CO wants me to check you out," the medic said, dropping his kit, "you were in the blast."

"I stayed out of the way." Teak concentrated on the medic's accent.

"We noticed." *English, but learned as a foreign language, probably in the States.*

Teak looked over the medic's shoulder and saw someone talking on a Thuraya sat phone.

"Does he want to talk?" asked Teak.

"Do you?" *No, maybe South African. But my ears are still ringing.*

Teak allowed the medic to examine him. He was older than Teak, thirty maybe, brown, his face covered in grime and stubble. He produced a penlight from one of his tactical vest pockets and shone the light in Teak's eyes.

"Anything you could do for any of them?" asked Teak.

The medic looked at Teak unhappily. "No," he said. Teak still couldn't place the accent. He could have been from anywhere.

"Have they found any uranium back there?" asked Teak, with an edge. But the guy was well-trained and said nothing. "Well, where you from?" said Teak. Light now, easy, friendly.

The guy smiled at him and walked away. *American?* Teak wondered where the medic had been last month.

In the center of the village the CO on the Thuraya walked a wide circle around the two survivors, who were under the guard of a black paramilitary in wrap-around Oakleys. The survivors were one of Hatashil's nephews, now relieved of his Enfield rifle, and the adolescent girl Teak had covered. Everyone else had either died in the blast, or taken up arms and been killed.

Then Teak saw the nephew make a run at the guy on the Thuraya. He had some kind of blade in his plastic-cuffed hands. The adolescent girl leapt for the black guard at the same moment. Teak watched the rest unfold in the elastic time that stretches and contracts around gunfire. It seemed to take forever for the guard to line up the nephew and then wheel back around on full automatic and hit the girl. But it had taken no time at all, Teak had only just jumped to his feet.

"Fuck," yelled the CO, throwing his arms up in the air, the Thuraya still in one hand. *American*.

5

David walked into Randolph Court to report to work. Randolph Court was a dormitory, part of Adams House. Franklin Delano Roosevelt had lived there. David thought about this as he picked up a mop and a bucket of chemicals from the basement. FDR had said his greatest regret in life was not getting into the Porcellian Club. At least that's what David had heard in the dining hall. And that Teddy had gotten in.

Back in the first week of school, David had joined dorm crew to make extra money. Dorm crew cleaned dormitories every other week, to supplement the maintenance staff. It was made up almost exclusively of international students on financial aid because, according to their student visas, they couldn't work for anyone except the university. The introductory meeting looked like an abbreviated European Union of reluctant janitors. A Scottish piano virtuoso, two Irishmen, half a dozen girls from Eastern Europe who were either short and stout like potato balls or tall and thin like dune grass on the Baltic. There was a Norwegian and an Israeli, both of whom had fulfilled their required military service before coming to Harvard and liked to talk about it. The Eastern European girls argued with the Israeli about which Web site was the best for buying Klubowes and Gauloises, yessmoke.com or internationalpuff.com. To his surprise David was the only African.

When they had been paired off, David's partner was the Scot. David, and everyone else, knew who the piano virtuoso was because the *Crimson* had run a profile of him after he had played the freshman talent show. He was a great, hulking young man, the color of the moon, almost albino. He looked more like a spiky haired rugby player than a pianist. His hands covered close to Liszt's two octaves. His name was Robert.

"Cleanin' up after rich wankers," he had said gruffly, "that's our job."

That morning, in Randolph Court, they started on the top floor. The first room had a sign on the door, Magic Marker and glitter on pink construction paper. It read:

The not-so-humble abode of
Prithee, Margo, Olympia, Carol

The girls' rooms were usually cleaner. David made it a point not to scrutinize the rooms he cleaned. Dorm crew was responsible only for the bathrooms, so he tried to stay in the bathroom, do the job, and get out. Robert, however, took an anthropological interest.

"Everyone in this place is identical," he shouted to David, who had gone directly into the bathroom. He rapped his knuckles on the wall through a Belle and Sebastian poster. The rooms in Adams House had dark wood floors, sepia walls, and exposed brick around fireplaces that the students were no longer allowed to use. And futons, televisions, books, posters. A certain kind of student, from Darien maybe, or Dubai or Los Angeles, bought an entire set of leather furniture and a plasma screen TV but most were less extravagant. Everywhere the digital detritus of the American upper middle class.

"Maybe that's a good thing, if we're all the same," said David, scrubbing out the tub. The ammoniac chemicals made his eyes water. "Maybe we're all the same so we'll get more done."

Robert came in to scrub out the sink. "We've always been the fockin' same and look where it's gotten us."

Robert was from a small town called Ayrshire, in western Scotland. It was remote. His father was a respected minister and a drunk. Robert was one of eight siblings. Of the other seven, six were still back in Scotland. His older brother had joined the army and, as Robert put it, "Gone to Iraq with fucking stupid Tony Blair's cock in his arse, and fockin' Bush's in his. Shite." Robert was generally pissed off, and confident that he was an order of magnitude smarter than anyone in his family. He could have gone to Juilliard or Guildhall, but unhappily figured that piano playing wasn't really a career. He was an economics major. He wanted to work at McKinsey when he got out of school and told David he'd never go home. David said he never wanted to go home either, even though he wasn't sure of this. By the end of their first day they had become friends. David never heard a single positive word from the Scot, but Robert was a consistent worker, and David respected that. The Eastern European girls, it seemed, mostly smoked and left unpleasant bathrooms completely untouched. He was glad he wasn't paired with one of them because he knew he would just do all the work himself.

* * *

The next room had no sign. As they opened the door there was a tin tumble as a pile of empty Budweiser cans fell to the floor. A large American flag hung on the wall over the fireplace.

"Fockin' Americans," said Robert, pausing in front of the flag.

"Patriotism," said David as he went to work on the toilet. The word did not exist in his family's native language.

"Patriotism my arse. This fockin' country wants to run the world." Robert looked around. In front of the window was a deluxe Moog keyboard. He stood over it and played Bach's fugue in G minor, the "Little," at double speed. He knew playing it would make David nervous. *Always sich a one fer the rules*. He turned off the Moog.

A door to one of the bedrooms was open. Robert stuck his head in. Extremely neat. A framed photograph of a thirty-one-foot sloop spraying white foam against an azure sky. A framed photograph of a team in Harvard rain gear, captioned "The Drinking Team That Sometimes Goes Sailing." On the window-sill, a tennis racket too old to ever be used again was positioned just so, like a window display, next to a small humidor. Made bed, fine plaid linens. Mohair blazer, seersucker suit, Brooks Brothers shirts in dry cleaning plastic, all hanging in the closet. Also in the closet, a glass bowl, half full of beer-bottle caps, mostly Heineken. Robert was about to laugh. Then, on the desk, he noticed a neatly stacked pile of envelopes and a calendar.

He called to David. David protested but then came to look.

"I think there's an invitation from every final club here," said Robert.

"Come on, Robert. We shouldn't be looking."

"It's a whole calendar's worth." Robert moved his finger from day to day on the desk calendar. Almost every other day that month had a punch event.

"Hey," a basso voice startled the two of them. "What the fuck are you guys doing in my room?"

Robert and David spun. Small for his voice, a curly blond student, fair and young in the face, yellow pants, powder blue shirt.

David was suddenly afraid. He never broke the rules. His whole school life he had been afraid of *being in trouble*. One afternoon, when he was a student in the great colonial house back home, in his excitement to get to cricket he had run out of form and taken a shortcut around the back of the house, past the flowing bougainvillea and uniformed servants and accidentally right into the master's afternoon tea. The master had been polite, but David knew that something bad was coming to him. What if they sent him home? He had privately burst into tears even though he was fifteen. That evening he had been told he was close to expulsion. When David remembered the incident later he knew they were just scaring him. But it did not matter. David did not like to be in trouble.

Before he could apologize to the furious deep-voiced boy, Robert said "We're just lookin fer an extra plug—"

"Get the fuck out of here," said the boy, pushing in front of them, hiding the calendar and invitations.

"Confidential information there?" said Robert.

"Jesus Christ, you guys are worse than real Mexican janitors."

* * *

Robert laughed about "real mexicans" the whole rest of the afternoon. David was quiet. The more David thought about that deep-voiced guy, the less funny it all seemed.

"Get any of those invites then?" said Robert, when they were dumping their boilersuits in the basement.

"One, to the Porcellian."

Robert had also received only that one.

"I reckon we'll see that fella there, too, then," said Robert, cheerily. He whistled Bach as they stowed the buckets and chemicals.

"Maybe he's not such a bad guy," said David

"He's a fockin' cunt."

They walked out of the basement into the ambitious twilight of the Yard. David went to the library. Robert went to Paine Hall and played Bach while he thought about quitting dorm crew and finding a job off the books somewhere. Maybe in a bar.

6

After she woke up and drank a latte and smoked a cigarette and took a shit, Jane walked to the intersection of Plympton Street and Massachusetts Avenue to meet her friend Sylvia, although *friend* is not exactly how Jane would describe her. Sylvia was really a Park Avenue girl, Jane thought, all pearls and Hamptons. *But she was down-to-earth in that discovered-nature-at-boarding-school-way, and had a sense of humor. It's not like Slyvia was a snob or anything, she just liked those pearls, and people should do what they like. And God, they'd known each other forever.*

Sylvia got famous early when her father, who was a partner at Goldman, rented all of Six Flags for her sixth-grade birthday party. Jane had gone because she was in New York for the weekend with her mother, an old friend of Sylvia's parents (*I know my mom fucked your dad*).

Jane and Sylvia walked to the *Crimson* through the early fall's quickening chill. There was going to be an editorial meeting to discuss taking a position on the alleged hetero-normative remarks made by Jada Pinkett Smith at a Black Student Association sponsored gala the week before.

"God, look at this," said Jane, staring at a girl in a three-quarter-length herringbone jacket, high heeling toward them over the narrow, cobblestone sidewalk.

"That's Amanda Clark," said Sylvia.

"She's the girl whose parents bought her the red Range Rover when she got early admission?"

"It was a Jeep."

"Big difference. My God, can you believe this place?"

Amanda was in front of them.

"Hiiiiiiii," said Sylvia. The greeting was five syllables. Amanda made the same noise.

"I'm having, like, the worst time. Hi Jane," Amanda said quickly, focusing her attention on Sylvia. "I'm going to check into the Charles for the night."

"What's wrong?" asked Jane with a mock sympathy that only Sylvia noticed.

"Fitz and I got into a big fight. I think I have to stay at the Charles for a couple of days."

The Charles was the best hotel in Cambridge. At the edge of campus, it was decorated in neutral colors but what the rooms lacked in character they made up for in boxy luxury and staff competence. Room service worked. Taxis came on time. There were two restaurants, Rialto and Henrietta's Table, where it was possible to purchase the same forty-dollar steak frites when parents were in town.

Jane held her tongue.

"Sylvia, would you come and have some dinner with me tonight? I just could use some support."

"I really have a lot of work to do," said Sylvia. Which was true. Sylvia was a strong student, spent whole nights in the library comparing and contrasting Walter Benjamin and Martin Buber, or analyzing the perspectival evolution of Piero Della Francesca. She had a lot of work to do. Also, she didn't want to agree to this decadence while Jane was there.

"We can have room service," added Amanda.

Sylvia finally agreed to call. They air kissed and Amanda continued in the direction of the hotel.

The rest of the walk to the *Crimson,* Jane thought about how, not so long ago, she would have loved to eat a third of a grilled cheese and two fried calamari off of room service china in the Charles. But not any more, she thought, I'm a different girl now. That girl back then never used to wonder why she got to stay in the Charles. It's not like she was a raving Marxist now or anything—it was so boring when people went on and on about politics—or even crazy, like that bald little Communist in her human rights class. But now she was aware. And at least she wasn't the same girl who cried when she didn't have anything to wear on her first day of college.

"Sylvia," she said as they walked through the red door of the *Crimson*. "Do you ever wonder when we'll stop being girls, like kids, and think of ourselves as adults?"

"Maybe when we're in grad school?"

The *Crimson* meeting was fun. The managing editor, Evan Krazmeyer, said he had some hard news, not the usual "bullshit celebrity stuff." Krazmeyer was from Beverly Hills and styled himself like an old news guy. He *woulda* worn a fedora if he *coulda* worked up the nerve. He settled for occasional suspenders, talking out the side of his wide mouth, and pulling at his unruly, curly hair with his stubby paws. He had gotten the top job more by dedication than talent. As Jane pointed out, "he *likes* sleeping in the office."

Krazmeyer began by knocking Jada Pinkett Smith down the docket. The new top story was about Africa.

"You gotta line on that, right Jane?" said Krazmeyer. Everyone knew about her boyfriend.

Africa was a big story on campus. The activist cause of the year concerned university divestment from an oil company with interests in the Horn.

"The great hero of the struggle," Krazmeyer explained, "is this guy Hatashil."

"He's an incredible story," said Jane. "He's an orphan who started a movement for independence from the Arab-dominated government after they killed his parents. But he's vowed that no innocents will suffer, like his parents did, when he's fighting. Sort of like a Robin Hood figure. He's way left, practically a Marxist. My boyfriend is from around there, and he says the guy is a hero, like, an actual one."

"But the story is," said Krazmeyer, "that his people went on a killing spree. So says Reuters. And the State Department just issued this release condemning him. So we need someone to do a story on the divestment group reactions. I'm thinking front page. We've had 'em there a lot recently. Now maybe we can wack 'em."

Jane was assigned the story.

"This is what Susan Lowell just won that Pulitzer for, too," she said.

"Maybe we can wack her, too," said Krazmeyer. "Knock those sunglasses loose."

The editors all laughed.

Walking out of the meeting into the cold it pissed Jane off when Sylvia called Amanda and agreed to eat room service and watch an on-demand movie.

7

Susan Lowell couldn't be sure, but she thought she heard a click on the line.

"Did you hear that?" she said.

"Hear what?" said Lunt. He was her best contact at the embassy in Nairobi and her third call that day. He leaned back in his chair and watched the waves of her voice manifest and roll across his computer screen.

"That 'tock' sound, soft?"

"You know how the phones are."

"Yeah, good, especially at the embassy."

"Power cuts this morning." *She's a sharp one,* he thought, not for the first time. "What can I do for you?"

"Have you heard anything about a massacre? Hatashil's people, up north?"

"Didn't you just win a Pulitzer?"

"So you haven't heard anything?"

Silence.

"Because first I heard that some of Hatashil's people were massacred, maybe even that he had been killed, and now Reuters comes out with this thing that *he's* been doing the massacring."

Lunt was silent again.

"Nothing? No ideas?"

"Haven't been out of the office in days, Susan."

Susan exhaled audibly and put her feet up on the sill of the window facing Annenberg, tapping the toes of her shoes on the glass. "Well, don't you worry Lunt, what's thirty lives in a war?" She said it flat, sarcastic, angry. "I'd kill that many people with my bare hands to get some answers today."

"No one's talking, huh?"

"Apparently no one in the whole of East Africa hears or sees anything. Did everyone decide to go on holiday for the last week, or what?"

"I don't know about you, but I only get two weeks a year."

Lunt was enjoying this, she could hear it. She could almost see him, his bulk spilling over his chair, looking out a window, over the barbed wire of the embassy, not looking at anything at all.

"Seriously, why the clamp down? Since when do you guys give a shit if thirty Africans get killed? I know you have a theory."

"No theories."

Susan sighed. She didn't know why, but she just didn't have it in her to keep pushing. She gave up. "All right, thanks Lunt," she said. "I'll be in touch." *Enjoy your two weeks, shithead.* She wondered why she had given up so easily. She never would have a year ago.

* * *

On the roof deck of her house in Beacon Hill, Susan Lowell lit a cigarette. The sky over Boston was cold and gray and promised changing weather. She was trying to quit. She was uneasy. What a stupid day.

She sat on the wooden table, thinking about the Pulitzer. The book was bulletproof, she was sure. The research was all there, she and Toma and Razi had nailed it. Hatashil's record had been perfect, the exception. She tried to imagine what could have happened to change the situation so radically.

The Pulitzer had been a long time coming. She had always worked harder than anyone she knew, harder even than her husband, Harry. He had started in the eighty-hour-a-week world of investment banking and it had worked out for him. He had moved on to become a partner at Dillon Associates, a mature hedge fund in Boston. He wouldn't have to work much longer if he didn't want to. He had made money, so that was that, he had already won.

But she had to work forever. It wasn't like banking and hedge funds, where you won by hitting your number and cashing out. To win in her game you had to be prolific, never quit. She had already done the unthinkable. Had two kids and won a Pulitzer. She was sure she would get tenure. And there it would be, another mythic obstacle she, Susan Lowell, had personally exploded. She hated listening to women complain about how it was hard, *unfair,* to be on tenure track and take time off for children. *Unfair? Who the fuck did these people think they were?* She knew she was a good mother.

Not that she had ever said this, or even really allowed herself to think it for more than a moment. It was unfair. She knew herself to be competitive, and lucky. Money. Big house, nanny, housekeeper. She and her husband laughed about the housekeeper, Ellie. She was a running joke. Harry didn't like Ellie, but she'd been working for them so long she had to stay. She sometimes brought her child, Jamal Jr., to the house. He was extremely sleek and dressed in toddler gangster gear. He was Ford's age, played with Ford's toys. When Ford had freaked out about this, Harry had sided with his son. Susan had thought it was good that Ford had to share with Jamal.

Their biggest amusement about it was that Jamal's father was also named Jamal, and Ellie complained about him constantly to her girlfriends over the phone, and to Jamal himself over the phone, and sometimes, though she usually held herself in check, to Jamal Jr. Susan and Harry had often paid higher phone bills because of Ellie's discussions about the Jamals, Jr. and Sr. Susan had occasionally walked into the living room to see Ellie, black hair spread like nappy seaweed over the gray couch, talking in pidgin St. Lucian on the portable phone. The phone bill rose again when she had dumped Jamal Sr. and taken up with another man, whom she insisted was just as good if not better. This new man's name was also Jamal. It was all hilarious to Susan and her husband. What was not hilarious was when Harry had found Jamal Jr. peeing on the carpet in his study.

Susan wondered from where, in Africa, all Ellie's Jamals were originally descended. Maybe Côte d'Ivoire. But it was so long ago you could never really know. She lit another cigarette off the first. Instead of a cocktail party to celebrate her Pulitzer, she would like to get drunk with Razi and Toma and then go home and get fucked by her husband. Then an image of David, her advisee, on top of her, flashed across her mind, and she mulled it over before dismissing the fantasy. The kid would be too scared.

Susan Lowell flicked her cigarette off the roof and watched it fall through the darkness to the street. She followed its descent, trying to figure out what was bothering her most. She walked back inside and to her office, where she scanned the bookshelves. On a whim, she pulled out a volume of T.S. Eliot's poetry. *Here I am, an old man in a dry month, being read to by a boy, waiting for rain.* She thought of Hatashil on a particularly cool night she had spent with him, when he had his boys practice English by reading an old missionary Bible to him. They had put down their Enfields and read Genesis, which was Hatashil's favorite. He was not a Christian, and neither was Susan.

And now I will never go back there, she thought. *What does it matter*. She had tried to go back six months before.

She had decided to stay at the new Nairobi Hilton to see what it was like. And it was close to the airport. She was only in town for two days, on her way north. Susan would always remember the red light flashing on the hotel phone, the breathy, heavy voice of the message telling her that fucking slick American girls should fucking go back where they fucking belonged if they didn't want to get hurt. She was embarrassed by how much it unnerved her. Without telling anyone, she had switched to the Stanley Hotel and tried to put it out of her mind.

The next day she had a coffee in the Thorn Tree Café like a tourist as she waited for Toma, with whom she was to have lunch. She was determined, in spite of the scare, to continue her trip, keep appointments. She watched the bustle. In front of the café, minivans and taxis discharged their passengers into the hands of bellboys in red and gold hotel uniforms. Blue-uniformed security guards with mirrors checked the undercarriages of the cars for bombs. Overweight businessmen in wide-lapelled suits spread by bulging guts laughed to Susan's right. A family of Swedes consulted a guidebook to her left.

In the middle of the café was an acacia which, so the story went, had been used by colonials as a message board since around the time Teddy Roosevelt had passed through on safari. All the current messages were from backpackers, Australians greeting their little brothers and recommending the Jockey Club, transient NGO kids looking for sublets, tourists warning other tourists off a particular guide at Kilimanjaro. Out of boredom, Susan left her drink and walked around the café's namesake, looking at the messages.

She was extremely surprised to see a sealed envelope with her name on it, tacked to the tree. She thought for a moment of Razi—it was the kind of thing he would do as a joke. Inside the envelope she found a photograph of a man she had interviewed for her book. One of Hatashil's lieutenants, whom Toma had introduced her to. In the picture he was tied to a tree in the desert. His face had been terribly bashed in, it looked like broken fruit, and on either side of him stood two young men grinning and brandishing heavy traditional fighting bracelets. On the back of the photograph was written "Go Home." Susan nearly retched.

Instead of returning to her room, she walked to the front desk and asked to use the phone. She called Milton Lambert. Lambert was a South African helicopter pilot who postured himself somewhere between mercenary and consultant as it suited him. She had met him at a party at the American embassy three years before. He had hit on her and given her his business card, which had a military looking head shot of himself printed on it.

Lambert was more than happy to come down to the Stanley on short notice to see the pretty American Harvard PhD student he remembered. He had heard of her success with the book, too, of course, how it had caused a bit of a stir, brought more scrutiny upon the National Security Front. He had read only the beginning. *No shit,* he had thought, the NSF tortures people and is corrupt as Amarulla left in the sun. Whether Hatashil was a freedom fighter, as she said, or just another bandit, well, that he didn't know. Didn't really, for that matter, care.

When he arrived at the Stanley he saw her to be almost as attractive as he recalled. "Change your mind about dinner?" he said, "Only took, how many years?"

She cut him off and showed him the threat and told him about the message at the Nairobi Hilton. He looked up, scanning the café.

"What do you think?" she had said.

"I think their intelligence people here don't fuck around. You should bloody well go home unless you've a good reason not to. What are you here for anyway?"

She didn't answer. She had wanted to get away from the kids, really, and from Harry for a bit, and have her own life again. So she had conceived of the trip as a magazine assignment, but really it was a vacation. She was putting herself in danger for fun. She was suddenly disgusted with herself, wished she could be teleported back to her roof deck on Beacon Hill.

Toma arrived late. He told them he had been followed. After that, Susan allowed Toma and Lambert to drive her to the airport. She boarded the next flight home feeling as though she had in some way disappointed her children. Or someone.

Susan had one more cigarette and left the roof, suddenly very cold. Down two floors she passed her own bedroom, where bedside light spilled out the door. Harry was asleep with a book on his chest. She knew that the alarm was set for six thirty and that when Harry woke up he would cook the children eggs but this did not make her feel anything but envy for what she perceived as his peace of mind.

Susan quietly opened the door to her daughter's room. *Can't remember childbirth, only the idea, not the pain. Wired that way so I'll have more.* She stood in the doorway looking at the sleeping child's pale face, blonde hair pooled around her cheeks on the pillow. Sometimes looking at a sleeping child was soothing and sometimes it was troubling and this time it was soothing. She looked at her daughter and was finally tired. Thankful, she crossed the hall, took off her clothing, turned off the lights, lay down next to her sleeping husband, and fell asleep herself. But she didn't know what she'd do in the morning.

Thousands of miles away, Deputy Political Counsel Lunt compressed Susan's voice, sent it off in an e-mail, and put his computer, which had been glowing with a picture of her face, to sleep as well.

8

The CO turned off the sat phone and watched the medic talk to the guy in the khaki suit. He wished that fucking Abdul hadn't blasted the kid. Shit happened, but that was unfortunate. It had just been a shard of Fanta can.

"What did the suit say?" asked the CO when the medic came back.

"He asked me if I could do anything for any of the villagers."

The CO looked at Teak leaning against his Land Cruiser in the distance.

"Then he asked me where I was from and if we'd found any uranium."

Smart ass.

The last of the sunset backlit a giant alto-cirrus formation in dark orange and pink. As the bomb crater faded into earthy black, Teak watched the CO approach, noting that he had a civilian haircut. He introduced himself as Blackford, just Blackford, and asked Teak who he was. Teak said he was an American with the Preservation Fund and had been driving north. He had stopped in the village because he had made the trip before and was friendly with the former inhabitants.

Blackford wished Teak were more shaken. But Teak stared coolly back at him. Blackford spoke in an articulate Southern drawl. "You asked my medic if we had found any uranium. Why?"

"I thought the U.S. Military had a sense of humor," said Teak. "But then," he said, cocking his head at Blackford, "I thought there were no Americans out here at all."

"There aren't, except for you," said Blackford.

Teak smiled. "So who are you guys?"

"I'm going to search you and your vehicle," said Blackford. He didn't know what to make of Teak and he didn't like not knowing. Searching, he didn't find the camera he was looking for. Teak didn't have one. Patting Teak down, he did find the SIG.

Teak said it was for the damn *shifta*. He hoped these guys didn't try to take him along when they left.

Blackford liked him, but if whoever the fuck he was had a mouth or was a *somebody* and ended up talking too much in Beijing or Paris or Beirut or Washington—that would be fucked. They had actually *reminded* him to be discreet on this operation. Well, there was nothing to do about that now. He would just let the guy go. But something didn't sit right. Maybe this guy was working for Hatashil. Maybe he should take the guy in, hold him till the right course of action became clear. Tie him up for a while.

"What did the kid have in his hands?" Teak asked.

Blackford sighed. "A shard of Fanta can."

9

David and Robert walked along a still and darkly green Brattle Street, by Georgian houses shadowed in the early moon. They saw another pair of young men in coats and ties ahead of them, scanning the houses for numbers. Glancing behind, Robert saw half a dozen more.

"If it's no good, we'll just get the fock out, aye?" said Robert.

"Yes," said David, knowing that he would not leave early.

An hour later, Robert picked up his fifth glass of pinot grigio and heard the opening notes of an old Sinatra standard. *Jazzy shite.* He followed the notes through the mahogany room. Half a dozen uniformed black men carried trays of hors d'oeuvres among the crowd of mostly young white men. Clouds of smoke rolled along the ceiling. Robert passed through the foyer, where a line waited to sign a large leather-bound guest register. Sliding his big frame through the line, he paused momentarily at the staircase to look at the banister. It was elegantly carved. The lines and curves reminded him of the best pianos he had ever played, like the Steinway at Sanders Theater at that freshman concert.

In the next room he found the piano, an upright against the far wall. Alumnus Jackson Oliver, his year's only black member, played and sang in a pinstripe suit. *Love was a kick in the head.* Robert was drawn to the piano. He inserted himself at the edge of the semicircle. Jackson was not a bad player. He stopped the song at "Like the sailor said" to sip his drink and light a cigarette. There were protests. He said he would finish after his smoke.

Robert recognized the deep-voiced blond guy who had told him to get the fuck out of his room. He was standing on the other side of the piano. They made eye contact and the guy quickly turned his attention to Jackson, saying his name, flattering him, asking how it was going at McKinsey.

"What's your name?" said Jackson.

"Spencer Edwards."

"You sure know a lot about me, Spencer, you CIA or something?" A couple other guys around the piano laughed. Spencer laughed with them, even though he was blushing. Robert could see how badly he wanted in with these guys, whatever in was. *Fock it, ah'll introduce mehself.* He turned to the guy on his right and did so. The guy said he was Peter. Peter was clearly drunk, swaying a little as he surveyed the scene. Peter was silent after he said his name.

"So, ehm, what's that?" said Robert, pointing at a green and white pin on Peter's lapel.

"Oh, it's just something we do. Excuse me." He walked off.

Christ. Robert downed his wine and decided to get another. On the way back to the bar he ran into David. They went to the bar together.

Jackson had gotten to the bar before them. He stood off to the side in conversation with Alan Green, an alumnus in his sixties who came to these events every year. Jackson was asking Green for news of Teak. When Jackson saw Robert and David, he motioned for them to come over. He introduced himself to both of them and then complimented Robert on his piano playing at the freshman concert. David was jealous of that connection. Then Jackson introduced them to Alan.

"We were just talking about Alan's godson Michael Teak, a good friend of mine. Who did you say he was working for?"

"The East Africa Wildlife Preservation Fund," said Green.

"Teak was one of the smartest guys ever to come out of this place," said Jackson.

"I don't know about that," said Green, "but he certainly ran a fast mile."

"I know some people who work for the Fund," David offered.

This was not exactly true. None of the white expat or scholarship children he had gone to high school with worked for the Fund. In his other life, however, growing up in his father's overcrowded and leaky house, he had known an older boy whose name was Moalana. On vacation from school, he had encountered Moalana hanging around outside the Fund's satellite office in town. Moalana told him he had run a package for them the week before, for a miraculous five dollars. He was hoping to do so again, by standing with the white NGO girl from Oregon who manned the office whenever she came outside to smoke cigarettes.

That was all David knew about the East African Wildlife Preservation Fund, but it was enough. At first, he and Alan

Green just talked about African wildlife. But then Green began asking David about the NSF, and then Hatashil. David was surprised at how much Green knew. Cocktail talk about Africa was usually short, but Green really knew. And more than that, he wanted to know David's opinion, what David knew. He asked David if he wanted to stay politically involved.

"I'm not involved at all."

"Everyone is involved one way or another, David."

"Not me."

"Well, we'll see. I'm on the board of the Boston Africa Action Group. You should come to a meeting."

Though David had no interest in this group, he said, "that would be great."

Abruptly, however, Alan Green shifted tones.

"You have a girlfriend?" he asked.

"I do, Jane Baker."

"Oh, I know the Bakers." Now he played the avuncular old man. "Pretty girl."

"Yes, sir," said David.

"What does she study?"

"She's concentrating on comparative literature but she really wants to be a journalist." David added with a touch of pride, "she worked at *Vanity Fair* last summer."

"Good," said Green. Then he took a card from his wallet, gave it to David, and said that his godson, Michael Teak, was an Africa expert, too, and that he hoped they could meet one day.

David was extremely pleased at this. After all, Green was an alumnus of the club. This would definitely help get him in. David looked at the card, which was heavy stock, white, and bore nothing but Green's name and contact information—in New York and Washington.

A little ways down the bar, Jackson spoke to Robert. "Every event, he's drunk" he said, indicating the guy wearing the pin, "Can you play any Satie?"

"Aye, but I never liked impressionism."

This cracked Jackson up.

"I'm just saying—"

"No, it's great," Jackson said. "Listen, go bop around. And talk to the guys in the green ties." He pointed down at his own green and white striped tie. Then he was gone, absorbed back into the crowd. Robert went back to the bar, where he found himself standing next to Spencer. Spencer shook his glass at the bartender over the table, spilling drops of Jack Daniels onto the white cloth.

"I asked for a Dewar's," he said.

"Christ," said Robert, drunk now and at peace with the fact. He glared at Spencer and ordered another wine.

"Excuse me?" said Spencer.

"Nice bottle-cap collection," said Robert.

"Have I done something to you?" asked Spencer, "do you have a problem with me?" He kept his voice down and tried to look like he was having a polite conversation, smiling as he asked the questions.

Robert was possessed of a keen and vengeful soul, but he realized that his instinct to punch Spencer over the bar was tempered by his desire to be in the club. Disgusted with himself he turned from the bar and walked to the piano.

The ritual of sitting down to play was usually important to Robert. This time, however, he sat down hurriedly. The room was full of young men who played the piano, decades worth of lessons. And although the men were of many different characters, the desire to show off was widely shared. Many of the piano players had thought about sitting down at the keys and showing off, because they rightly suspected that the club valued the ability to play at dinner parties, but they weighed this against being the guy to show off and calculated that it was better to play it cool because this was the first event.

Alan Green saw all this in their faces as he watched the big Scot sit down heavily at the piano. Even drunk, he was clearly a brilliant player. Such were the reasons, Green reflected, that he came to these things. All the young men were remarkable. There was a strange and pathetic nostalgia in how he was still so wired into this scene, he knew, but he didn't look at that part of it directly. His visits were in their way informal recruiting trips. Talent spotting, that archaic practice. He liked watching the young men try to figure things out, he liked guessing what they were thinking. When he himself had started, it had been the happiest time in his life, and the romance of the Cold War still remained with him. It was all just so much damn fun. He wondered if they had as much fun now and suspected not. *Too fucking bad*. He'd be damned if he was going to be another old man wistful for the Cold War. He'd just have to keep things interesting.

Robert ran his large pale hands up and down the keyboard. A sonata of his own composition at high volume. He knew that much of the room was looking at him and listening intently. The piano was slightly out of tune. He thrashed his head like a

Beethoven caricature and *played the shite* out of the piece. He thought about Spencer and confirmed again for himself what he knew about being a piano player, which was that when you played angry, the music was angry.

"Hey, Beethoven," said Spencer, who had sidled up to the piano with some new friends. "It's not a funeral in here." Spencer's friends, a pair dressed like him, in tweed, laughed hard, and the laughter spread like an infection to a couple of surrounding members and punches.

Robert stood up from the piano and loomed over Spencer.

"What, you want to *fight*?" Spencer's blond, curly hair seemed to glow as he chuckled, and Robert realized, through his anger, that they were the center of attention, that he was the butt of the joke. He looked across the room to where David was still in conversation with Alan Green. David had noticed the exchange and decided that he would not look over there, and *damn, Robert, why did he have to go and do such a thing?* And then Robert was at his side, interrupting Alan Green, who was telling a story about a murder in New Haven.

"Come on, David," said Robert. He was clearly drunk and David watched nervously as Alan Green noticed this. "Let's get the fock oota here."

David hesitated for a moment and then he said, "Actually, Robby, I think I'll stay for a bit longer." He didn't mean to call him Robby. Or know that the diminutive would produce the vertical, blank, expression on Robert's face that it did. "But I'll see you soon."

But then Robert was gone.

As Green introduced him to some other young men David thought about how he and Robert were friends and how Robert wouldn't really care that he was staying on for another drink. And after a few minutes he had almost convinced himself that he hadn't seen that look on Robert's face.

10

One of the reasons Teak went to Harvard was to run. An all-state middle distance runner, it was his plan to run for the school. But by the fall of his sophomore year he was consumed by his language studies and from then on he ran only for himself. At first he tried running at the Hemenway gymnasium at the law school, widely regarded as the finest gym available to the nonvarsity population, and very convenient with his class schedule. The treadmills at Hemenway, almost continuously occupied, were sleek, black, and almost silent, expensive tools with flat-screen televisions affixed to each, showing premium cable—almost always the news.

On his first visit Teak stood in the back of the room, next to the white, Olympic regulation squash courts, and watched his fellow students run in place as they watched stock footage of IEDs exploding, and then a reporter in flak jackets over button down shirt. Teak changed into gym clothes and ran very hard for an hour. Everyone around him was fit. No one made eye contact, although the place pulsed sex with every damp ponytail bounce. It was the same the next day, and the next, and until it struck Teak that if he returned again, he would see the same people running in the same place, watching more or less the same news, and from then on he ran outside whatever the weather. He said the physics of treadmills was no good, but what he could not get out of his head were the parallel tracks of hapless war and running in place.

The cold came very early that fall, which was fine with Teak. He did not listen to music while he ran, rather he thought about language, collateral damage, what he knew and did not know, and how he had to study harder, run harder, fuck harder. And he ran and ran, and one wet evening after a dense rain there he was, was almost sprinting the foggy fluorescence of the last mile of the path along the Charles River, and then over the bridge, high kneeing over the river. *It's hard but I like it.*

He spat over the rail and slowed to a trot from the river back to Adams House. Charlie Atwater, the rangy former president of the Porcellian whom he had met once before, at a tailgate at the Yale game, was standing under an eave on the corner, smoking a cigarette with a couple of other club members.

"You are one tough motherfucker to be running in that," said Charlie Atwater.

"Not really," said Teak, knowing that it would be much colder in the new year. He could see himself in the dark and cold, running miles along the Charles, to Watertown and back, or into Boston and back.

"So what do you know about Washington in July?" Atwater asked, and invited Teak out for a drink. Teak changed into dry clothes and they went to Daedalus and talked about summer internships. A friend of Charlie's had an apartment nearby and after Daedalus closed they went there. It was a kind of informal punch event. Teak noticed that Atwater asked a lot of questions about his godfather, Alan Green. At the end of the night, when Atwater was drunk, he said, "no surprise you run in the cold, Green is a fucking legend."

Teak, who admired his godfather, thought about this. He felt a twinge of unease, as though, perhaps, being part of a legend might not be *better,* might not be *harder,* might not be right. But he didn't know what would be better. Mostly, he felt pride. The other club members, drunk to a man, nodded whether they knew what Atwater was talking about or not.

11

Jane wanted a full report, so David met her at Shay's. She was with a lot of people, as usual, sitting outside in the sharp pre-winter so they could smoke. David noticed the journalist friend of Professor Lowell's, a couple tables away, but couldn't remember the guy's name

Razi sat alone. He had been thinking about an old story and suddenly was distracted by the tall black guy. He knew him but couldn't place him. It didn't matter. Razi was feeling sorry for himself again, peeling back the years.

His first big story had been about the son of the head of Saudi Intelligence who had betrayed his father and fled Jeddah with twenty million dollars embezzled from one of the Islamic banks his father advised. And then the son, named Aziz Al-Emudi, had vanished. Great story. Oxford educated and a favored son, his betrayal had come as a dangerous surprise within the tight-knit Saudi elite. Razi broke it all. But then the story was over, and Razi's star fell, plateaued, and drove him to obsessive research on that first, shining success. He discovered nothing new and was forced to conclude, like the rest of the world, that Al-Emudi had disappeared into a life of quiet luxury, somewhere in Europe probably. But that had never sat right with Razi. It was about a year after Al-Emudi vanished that he slowed down on his reporting and began drinking. Then less and less reporting, more drinking. That is, until Toma had introduced him to Susan, so they could work on Hatashil. He'd sobered up for a while. Until the story was over.

Razi suddenly remembered. The kid was one of Susan's advisees. He watched David talk and tried to listen.

David described the punch cocktails to Jane but wished, when he was done, that he had not told her about Robert in quite such detail. But the mad piano playing would make the rounds anyway. He was still nursing his first beer when he saw Jackson Oliver walking down the block toward Shay's with an angular but pretty ash-blonde girl on his arm. The ash-blonde girl called out to Razi and she and Jackson stopped on the sidewalk in front of the tables.

Razi watched the girl as she made her way to him. Jackson followed her movements, too, and, after a moment, noticed David and said hello to him.

"You want a smoke," he asked David and lit up while the ash-blonde told Razi how much she was enjoying his seminar.

"Yeah, sure," said David, and went to stand with him on the sidewalk although he didn't smoke. Jane raised her eyebrows but said nothing. David corrected himself as Jackson held out the pack. "Actually, I don't smoke." He was nervous but recovered. "I just wanted to stretch my legs and say hello."

Jackson laughed. It seemed to David that Jackson laughed at everything.

"Yeah, it's good to talk," he said. "Your pal Robert really plays that piano."

"Robert, yeah, he had a few drinks."

Jackson, smiling for effect, reclaimed his Queens grammar school syntax. "I don't know how a nigga can get through that shit sober. But you had a good time?"

David was, as always, stunned by the use of the word nigger.

"Yeah, yeah," David said to Jackson, feeling sweat on his palms. "It was a little strange, but I enjoyed it."

"It's good to talk to people like Alan Green," Jackson said, suddenly almost solemn. "That's what this place is about, that's the education. The professors. The people you get access to. That's what you have to soak up at that stupid punch shit." He flicked the cigarette away as the ash-blonde said good-bye to Razi and joined them. Jackson did not introduce her.

"So, maybe I'll see you at the next one?"

"Absolutely," said David, his mind racing. *Was it a tip, a guarantee about the first cut?* Jackson and the ash-blonde continued down the street. David sat back down with Jane.

"You don't smoke," she said.

"I didn't," he said. "I was only saying hello."

She could see that he had liked the event. She derided the clubs again, but not out of any meanness, she told herself, only out of instinct and reason, recounting the story of a friend of a friend who had been taken to one of the rape rooms.

David just looked at her. The table went quiet.

"They call it that themselves," said Jane. "Sometimes they're joking but you know how that goes." As Jane told the story David registered in her eyes actual horror, and beneath that, fear. Jane had been pawed enough to know the panic of being pushed up against a wall, the possibility of rape. She had slapped a boy, a big football player who had cornered her in a stairwell her freshman year. And the shelter where she worked an afternoon a week was for abused women. But she prided herself on not wearing any of that on her sleeve. All the *take back the night* grandstanding by girls in tight pants irritated the shit out of her. She was wary of those moments when, in discussing the sexual aggression of her peers, she had sexualized herself, made herself more attractive in the conversation. It was a third date thing. Usually she was icier and shrewder and more respectful. So she continued clinically.

"You know about the door, right?"

David didn't. None of the boys at the table did, but all the girls nodded.

"Yeah. In the girl's bathroom in the Science Center basement one of the stall doors is covered in notes. There must be what, thirty or forty of them? They all say things like 'I was raped in the Fly, Fall 05' or 'Phoenix Winter 04' or 'AD Spring 03.' Or whatever."

Razi watched Jane and her table of undergraduates, and thought about what he had lost since he had been a student. At times he had been like them. Bright, loud, a lot to say. When he had traveled with the Tigrayan People's Liberation Front in Ethiopia he had been young, and so were they, and it seemed almost like their revolution could have been his revolution. One of the guerrilla generals had given him a copy of their *Revolutionary Democratic Sex Manual*. The general was very serious about the book, which proscribed rules for men's brigades and women's brigades. Unmarried fornicators were to be stoned to death, for example, as there was no room for fornication at this point in the revolution and bullets were too valuable to waste on fornicators. Razi had accepted the gift seriously but joked about it relentlessly with the soldiers when he was away from the commanders. He still treasured the delicate, rain-warped book, ran his hands over the brown goatskin cover. It was just so damn funny. He loved to tell people about it.

After that story was over, Razi decided to look up the manual's author, and was surprised to find that he lived in London. He was a round man, his syrupy Tigrayan face pocked and spectacled. When they met, the author was seated at a table outside the pub, *much as I am seated here at Shay's,* thought Razi. It turned out that the author didn't care, really, about sex or the revolution. At least that's what he had told Razi.

"I fought a war for the country but I always knew that I didn't want to stay," he said at the end of their interview.

"So why did you write the book?" asked Razi. "They all call you one of the fathers of the revolution."

"It was the only book I could write in the bush," he said, lifting the last of his ale to his lips. "I always wanted to be a poet."

Razi hadn't believed him at the time. But there at Shay's, watching Jane talk about rape, he suddenly changed his mind.

12

In the darkness the stars slowly brightened and Teak stood in the center of the largest crater in the village. The paramilitaries had left, but Teak had stayed. He looked to the east where they had driven off, into the now soft blue-black of an empty plain. Kneeling, he picked up a handful of the blasted dirt and brought it to his nose. It smelled of nothing but dirt—no blood, no ash. He was tempted to say something into the air on behalf of the people who had been killed, but he could not think of anything, and then it wasn't his right anyway, he thought, to say anything like that. He let the dirt trickle from his hand and took his phone from his pocket. He accessed his address book, whose first entry was "Atwater, Charlie."

Teak nearly called Atwater, but then took a breath. It seemed like those paramilitaries had been American, but that, he thought, could not be. He returned the phone to his pocket. He squinted now into the darkness, since the electric light of the screen had shrunk his pupils. He took another deep breath and began walking a circle around the crater.

Teak had developed a trick in college for speaking with authority. When he decided to talk in class, he would often begin by saying something like "there are really three important points." Even if he didn't know what the points were, he'd come up with them. He believed that breaking his argument into numbers forced people to pay attention. How you said something could be more important than what you said, he figured, and used his point system even though it occasionally made him feel like a fake.

One, he thought. Americans. The medic, the gear, and the CO, Blackford, his accent. American for sure. The rest, Africans.

Two. I am an American.

Three. A hit on the village without my knowledge is a hit on me.

So they couldn't have been Americans. Because we don't kill each other.

Teak knew his history, he had studied betrayal after betrayal between citizens of the same nation. That's what drove history. But he also knew that if he operated under the assumption that he was expendable, then he could not do his job. And he thought of his godfather, his family in the Agency. Then he thought about Joint Special Operations Command, JSOC as he had seen it written on the odd document, though he had never heard JSOC discussed.

He opened his phone again and looked at Charlie Atwater's phone number.

The year before Michael Teak was a freshman, Charlie Atwater had been president of the Porcellian. It was common knowledge, after his graduation, that Atwater had gone on to be some kind of special forces guy. Most people thought it was SEAL but everyone in the Porc, at least everyone who cared to follow such things, knew that he was army and that he had jumped right out of Ranger school into Delta. The SEAL weren't for him. In a swim rescue test he had suffered a swimming induced pulmonary edema (a SIPE), passed out, and had to be fished out of the tank, nearly dead. After that he was recycled into Delta and made the cut, thirteenth of the thirteen accepted candidates from the original pool of one hundred. Teak heard rumors that Atwater had only gotten the second chance because his father, who ran a consulting firm with Giuliani, employed a half dozen former Delta guys at the top of the security division and they were still wired in. But who knew. Teak was also planning to serve his country and had resolved never to suffer a SIPE, though he did not know what preventative measures he might take.

They had been introduced at the Game, the annual football match between Harvard and Yale. Teak remembered it clearly because Green had called him by his last name, which was strange. "Teak," Alan Green had said, "come over here and meet Atwater."

The Porcellian, like all the other clubs, drove buses and SUVs to the game for the elaborate tailgate. The Porc tailgate was a high point of the year for the members and younger alums, who showed up together in small groups, seldom with girlfriends or wives. Alan Green always tried to go, looked forward to it every year. The deferential, curious young men, the fall afternoon, the *pork.* He lived in a house full of women—none of them had ever gotten football.

Unlike Green, Charlie Atwater had returned that year only because of the SIPE. He was a famous jokester and loved the rumors swirling around him. He played the secret agent part with wry, vain intensity. Teak remembered him doing a backflip when a firecracker went off in the parking lot.

Teak was not even in the club yet, but he had known several members from Buckley and then Exeter and elsewhere. Green had already introduced him to a lot of people who were at that tailgate, some punches. One in particular, Jackson Oliver, often invited him out. The handsome Guyanese had slid into the Ivy League world like cuff links thrown over ice, by way of a prep-for-prep program that had brought him from public school in Astoria to private school in Manhattan. He didn't know where he was going exactly, but he was resolved to have a good time. He thought Teak was too serious, but also that he never took anything for granted. "And," Jackson had said to Teak early on, "these are some spoilt motherfuckers 'round here. Know what I mean?" Teak did. It was part of why he wanted to serve.

"*Ratatatat,*" Jackson had said to Charlie Atwater after the game, as they and Teak and a couple more guys and one or two of their girlfriends sat around a table on the first floor of Daedalus. "Is that how they come after you, Chuck? *Blat blat*?"

"Yeah, sort of like that," Atwater fired back. "Like on the hard streets of Astoria."

It was rude and charming at the same time. Teak was interested in Atwater's training. There was something about Atwater that distinguished him from everyone else sitting around the table. A certain toughness, and this also made Teak want to serve.

* * *

Charlie Atwater wasn't the best shot in his chalk and Baghdad wasn't easy, but he was fine for a rookie. *Careful.* The whole time he had been scared. Of all the horrors that lay in the wings of urban warfare, he had a special fear of the concrete chips that flew off the walls of the alleys under fire. Something about how small they were, how inconsequential. Because he was afraid that one would fly right into his eye like a dart, he never took off his goggles. And when he had clocked enough time, *done his duty,* when he wanted out, a better job, he called Alan Green for advice.

The last time Teak saw Atwater, Teak was having breakfast by himself in Daedalus, reading the paper. He glanced up at the television, tuned to CNN. A new special envoy to Iraq was boarding a helicopter in the Green Zone, and who was behind him but Charlie Atwater. It made perfect sense to Teak. He was as well trained as any bodyguard. Though he had been a shitty student, Charlie Atwater did have a degree in government from Harvard, and he could be extremely charming. Teak could see him at the embassies, chatting up the journalists. Teak figured the envoy was glad to have him and imagined half a dozen connections that could have placed Atwater there. Teak was uneasy, however, seeing Atwater on television, in a position of power in the Green Zone because he was really just a kid. *Like me,* thought Teak. He hoped they were good enough to do the work. If anyone had ever put the question to him, of course, he would have said yes without hesitation.

In the village, Teak stepped up out of the shallow crater, looking at Charlie Atwater's phone number. He hit call.

13

That next afternoon was immaculately clear but David was too excited about his meeting to enjoy the weather. He liked going to Professor Lowell's office in the Knafel building. The steel, light wood, and clear glass declared a quiet safety and professionalism that appealed to him. There was nothing like it at home. He thought, going into the building, that he was on the right path to something even if he did not know what. Especially after last night. The punch event went great. He even had a question about it to ask Professor Lowell. It was all connected, he was sure.

"Come in," she said at his knock.

Susan Lowell liked David. For one thing, she liked looking at him, as he gracefully lowered his long body into the chair in front of her desk. She also liked David for his formality. In their first meeting he had shown her where his family's village was, on the map on her wall, and she had marked the spot with a yellow tack. But after that he never spoke about his personal life, only about classes and politics. Even in discussions about his country, the rebellions, and Hatashil, all the subjects of her work thus far, he never mentioned his family to her, though she knew everyone in Southern Somalia, in the region, really, was touched by the NSF. David was shrewd and did this purposefully, to keep the famously cool Professor Lowell's attention. He hoped to know her for a long time.

As was her custom, she busied herself stacking papers as they began talking.

"Did you know a boy a few years older than me named Teak?" asked David. "I think he spoke Kiswahili."

"He spoke Amharic and Arabic and some others, too," she said, without looking up. "But I didn't know him myself." She knew more about him than that. In the young-professor gossip nexus, Teak had occupied a prominent position. Lowell didn't engage much in the ubiquitous talk about the students—whose father was which senator, who had slept with whom—but even she had become interested in Teak. For one, he was squarely, nondescriptly, handsome. Tall and blond, the kind of boy she had dated in college. And in his four-year universe he stood out for other reasons, too. He was an all-Ivy miler before he quit to accommodate his extra courses. His remarkable facility with languages, of course. Spoke rarely in his seminars but aced every class. Never lingered to bullshit with the professors, which was de rigueur for ambitious students who said things like de rigueur. Wrote a publishable thesis, she had heard, something about linguistics and foreign policy. It had won a Hoopes Prize. He was rumored to have slept with several of the teaching fellows and have a pilot's license. She was always surprised that such people existed. But then, she was one of them, except for the mile and the pilot's license.

"Why do you ask?" she said now, looking directly into David's open face.

"Just curiosity, really," he said, slightly unnerved. "I met someone who knew him."

He had been thinking, since the punch, about what Jackson had said about access. That's what the professors were here for. They were adults, and David was supposed to be an adult. They weren't the teachers at his school back home, he didn't have to call them sir. Here they were all supposed to belong to the same great university.

But now that he had brought Teak up, he didn't know what else to say. He retreated to talk of his paper for her seminar, which was an analysis of American news coverage of his home and the NSF. David's problem was that he was no good at writing essays, and this was a twenty-plus-page assignment. He had not had a computer in high school and he had never written anything longer than a couple of handwritten pages. His freshman year had been a torturous succession of all-nighters trying to structure his ideas the way they demanded in expository writing—expos—the dreaded freshman requirement. Some of his peers wrote their essays in under an hour. He knew they had been practicing since they were seven years old, but that didn't make him feel any better. Jane wrote her papers drunk if she felt like it. She helped him with his assignments on occasion, but more often offered and forgot, or started to help, became distracted, and they ended up fucking.

And then, when David was accepted into Professor Lowell's seminar, Lowell had said to "forget expos." David couldn't believe it, and he was very happy, if a little confused. Susan Lowell knew exactly what she was doing. When she read the hundred applications for her thirteen-person seminar, her book was in its third printing and controversial. David's application confirmed her most vitriolic condemnations of the NSF—the Mogadishu-bred, mutating, ruthless security agency—and also her support for Hatashil. Hatashil and the NSF had grown up simultaneously—*they even went transnational at the same time,* Susan had thought wryly. So David was a good omen. She not only let him into the seminar, she become his academic advisor. That she knew about his home and cared about it was both balm and salt to his homesickness.

They spent most of their meetings simply working on how to write an essay. They always agreed about content. When they had first talked politics they recognized in each other a manifest hate of the NSF that came from familiarity with the details. In particular, they loathed Hassan Al-Kateb. In the measured tones of academics, they discussed his torture squads, his use of airplanes, his notorious womanizing. But they never became heated, though they spoke of blood. Getting angry, or even sarcastic, was the mark of an amateur.

Today, however, Susan Lowell was angry. Her thoughts wandered as she looked at David. She had spent the morning on the phone. Weirdly, no one at Reuters could tell her who had written the story about Hatashil's so-called massacre. No one at the State Department was authorized to discuss their statement. All the press officers seemed to be at an early lunch together. It was like the story and the statement had simply *appeared* in the media, materialized out of the ether. And Razi had been no help. She had asked him to look into it, but she had a feeling he wasn't doing much of anything. She tried to focus on David.

"What do you make of the news about Hatashil?" She asked him. David hadn't heard, so she explained the reports of the massacre.

"I don't believe it," David said.

"I don't either," she said, "but—" her cell phone rang. It was her nanny, telling her she needed another few days in New York. Susan clenched her jaw and began rearranging her schedule in her head. It would be a hassle to pick the kids up every day. *Another problem*. She hung up the phone, pushed her feet into the floor beneath her desk, and took a deep breath.

"Professor?" David was tentative. "Is everything okay?"

"Don't you just hate him, David?" she said. "Al-Kateb."

David didn't know what to say.

"You know, I had a fixer when I was over there, named Toma Mugabo, who became a friend of mine. He used to say this thing about Al-Kateb. It went 'I'll believe in anything if you'll believe in anything.' Because Kateb was a Muslim but a bad Muslim. I think that was the point of the saying. What do you think?"

Jesus, thought Susan right after she said it. *I can't believe I said that to him.* Whenever she said too much, the words sat in her stomach for days. She had always thought she would grow out of that.

She watched David shift in his chair.

David dropped his eyes from Professor Lowell and thought of his one serious encounter with the NSF. He knew many stories, of course, but had only personally banged up against them this one time. At the airstrip. When David was eleven, there was this *mzungu* girl from Oregon on a six-month ICRC posting and she had adopted a stray dog. An Ethiopian wolf that became very sick.

That day she was at the airport, which was just a strip and a building with a tin roof, close to where David lived. A dozen members of an illegal local militia, some with ties to Hatashil's then-nascent movement, sat in the shade of the single building. They were bullshitting and gambling, the butts of their Kalashnikovs resting in the dirt. David usually stayed away from them.

The Oregon girl was seeing off an ICRC team about to fly food to the Nuba Mountains. David and his father had been passing the airport when Moalana, a slightly older boy who sometimes worked for the Oregon girl, had run, spindly limbs awhirl, from the girl's side to their truck. He wanted to see if David's father, a veterinarian, could do anything for the dog, which had just collapsed. They had turned the truck around and David's father examined the dog. David stood behind his father, watching the aid workers load the plane, wondering about flying.

And then a cloud of dust had risen in the distance. Before David understood what was happening, several NSF trucks had arrived and the militia had taken up positions around the building. The girl sprinted for the plane and the aid workers yelled at each other to leave the supplies behind, one even left his hat and sunglasses on top of a crate. They ran to the plane, piled through the door, and the last one in slammed the hatch behind them. The NSF shot at the plane as it accelerated forward. *Why shoot something, made of metal,* David had thought, *that can fly!* Then his brain had shut down and he had run with his father back to the truck and driven off down the road, parallel to the runway. David watched out the window as three bursts of rounds popped around the airplane, striking earth and gravel into the air. They were shooting at the wheels. Behind him, several militiamen lay bleeding in the dirt. The rest had scattered. The last thing David saw was an NSF guy flipping his rifle to automatic and exploding the dog.

David could not fall asleep that night. His father had sat in a chair next to his bed, almost until dawn. "The dog was going to die anyway," he had said.

"I'm not sure what the expression means, Professor Lowell," David said now, deciding that honesty was best. Proverbs were difficult in a second language and he wondered if Professor Lowell could ever get it. He wanted her to, and he wanted to tell her the story of the dog, but didn't. Instead he said, "maybe the reporter got the story wrong."

"I hope so," she sighed. "Let me know if you hear anything from back home, okay?"

David was pleased with the assignment. He didn't think he'd actually hear anything. But that didn't matter. What mattered was that he was getting closer to Professor Lowell. He was moving further along the path.

14

The night was moonless, but the starlight was now bright and illuminated the dry dirt beneath Teak's boots as he walked the cracked plain. He held his phone to his ear and followed one fissure to another.

The call went through to Charlie Atwater but was sent straight to voicemail.

"Hey Charlie, Teak here. I ran into an old friend of yours. Let's catch up." *He'll call back.*

Teak himself always answered his phone if he could. Always returned e-mails and voicemails as soon as he received them. It was an aspect of loyalty, and everyone he knew picked up on it. It was one of the reasons people liked Teak. Throughout college he had witnessed the ragged band-saw arguments that divided lovers and friends and roommates, but he had never lost anyone that way. Teak had never had a *falling out* with anybody. When Charlie Atwater and Jackson Oliver talked about him, as they talked about everyone in their club, they discussed his loyalty. They also discussed the way he talked, his use of language.

"Weird," Charlie had told Jackson.

"Sort of like an old man," said Jackson.

It wasn't quite that, but Jackson didn't know what to call it. They were talking about the eccentric notions that Teak, though generally quiet, sometimes expressed out of the blue in the endless club and bar and dorm bull sessions. Like what Teak was thinking right then as he returned to his Land Cruiser and looked back over the destroyed village. He might have said it over a beer at Daedalus.

Gods of which I know nothing.

After Blackford's unit had taken off, Teak had driven another half mile downstream, parking among the low rocks for cover. He was planning on leaving before daylight. In the meantime he could see the village clearly through his night-vision scope. Still nothing, only the bodies where they had fallen.

Teak put down the monocular and lit a cigarette. His thoughts kept spinning. *You can slide right in and disappear into your own head*. As if every decision he had ever made was connected to the dark blood on the dirt. He pushed the thoughts away. *Upstream*.

The bomb had blown pieces of the huts a hundred meters down the stream bank. One piece of wood had stuck like a javelin in the earth. *Deconstruction. That was what my entire education was about.*

Teak turned the NOD up to the sky, where the stars now looked like white pinpricks against a great green sheet. *We were taught to think critically.*

Teak's phone rang, an alien sound out there. It was Charlie Atwater. Teak walked away from his truck, exchanging pleasantries under the giant sky, looking at the bombed-out village. Atwater had no idea where Teak was. At first they talked about girls they knew in college. Atwater had seen that cute English PhD candidate, Amy, at a party last time he was in New York.

Finally, Atwater said, "so what's this about some old friend of mine?" He was sitting on the steps of the Capitol building, on lunch break from his new job as a lobbyist for an oil company. The Defense Department, it had turned out, wasn't that much fun. And while most days Atwater enjoyed expensive lunches, once in a while he liked to take a walk around the Capitol building, get a BLT, and eat it outside. That's what he was doing.

"Who was it?" Atwater asked through a mouthful of extra bacon.

"Blackford. Remember him?"

Atwater was quiet on the line.

"Charlie? You there?" asked Teak.

"Where'd you meet him?

Something's there. Something.

"Just in a bar over here. Seemed like a smart guy, had had a few, and when I mentioned Harvard he said he knew you. Anyway, I wanted to see if you had any contact info for him, he left his Red Sox cap at the bar."

"You know, I'm not sure I know him. Name just sort of rings a bell. Sorry I can't help. Anyway, listen, I've got to run."

Too quick.

"All right," Teak said. "Let's get together when I'm back in the states. Have some drinks."

On this topic Charlie Atwater was once again enthusiastic. They would meet in New York next time they were both there.

Teak sat and thought and looked at the stars. Knowing he wouldn't be able to sleep yet, he checked the news on his phone. He was surprised to find reports of a massacre perpetrated by Hatashil on the wires, and even stranger, a statement from State, with Intelligence Czar Mitchell Harrison the first man condemning it.

When he finished reading, Teak knew he wouldn't be able to sleep at all. He thought, *Isn't that supposed to happen when you see children killed.*

15

David was startled to attention by a sharp knocking at his door. He had been at his desk with his face in John Stuart Mill's *On Liberty*. Jane leaned against the doorjam in jeans and a striped T-shirt.

"I have to keep reading," he said.

"Okay."

But as she lay on the bed, fully clothed, looking up at the ceiling, her hands behind her head, he could no longer concentrate. She cracked a smile when he stood up from his chair and walked over to the bed, but she didn't turn her head.

In bed, after, he lay staring out the window.

"You really ought to get a double bed," she said.

"I don't need one," he said. And then, "do you think I'll get in?"

She went to the window and smoked a cigarette out into the night. "Probably not," she said.

"Why?"

But she would not tell him. It made him furious. And more determined. The fall air blew over David's face and he closed his eyes. The smell of wet leaves on the breeze and her on his pillow mingled in his nostrils with the smoke. Few at home smoked anything but pipes, as cigarettes were expensive. Many chewed khat. He never did. *She ought to answer my question,* he thought.

"Did I tell you I'm going to Kenya?" she spoke out the window.

"No." *Definitely not.*

"My anthro professor turned me on to a conference in Nairobi," she said.

She waited till she was drunk to tell me this.

"I'm not sure if I've got the invitation for sure, but no matter what, I'm going in a few weeks. I was talking with my parents about it—they had been planning a safari thing anyway so it'd be totally dumb not to go."

"In the middle of school?"

"Yeah, that's why this conference would be good. Like a working vacation."

"What'll you do?" *She must have known for months.*

"A story for the paper. Compare literatures." She laughed. "I don't know. But this way it's not so much like just playing hooky, you know?"

There was something about the way she said this that angered David. He wanted to call her *spoiled*. But really he wanted her to apologize for not telling him, for not letting him into this life of hers. He decided he wanted to fuck her again. She would do whatever he wanted in bed. This time very fast,

David angry, Jane arching, surprised. It made him feel better, but only for a moment. Then he felt worse again.

And then she asked him about Hatashil.

"Must be some mistake," he said. He didn't want to talk about it.

"I don't think so," Jane countered. "And you know what, I think your professor girlfriend might be in big trouble. They were talking about how the Pulitzer people were going to investigate her book. They could take it away from her. I'm doing a story on it."

"Maybe you can do some reporting on your *working vacation,*" said David, rolling over.

"Maybe I will."

Outside, they heard final club boys singing to each other.

"Sounds like they're playing army," whispered Jane in the darkness.

16

Their voices were hoarse from singing, and their heads ached from last night's cheap beer, but Lucas and Willy were drinking again. *Babababam KABOOM*. Lucas thought if he had a real Uzi he might be able to make that red Jeep explode. He sat on the steps of the *Lampoon* in the easy evening and swished a glass of Maker's Mark and ginger ale. Lucas didn't really want blood, he wanted comedy. He wanted more weed.

"Why is it," said Lucas to Willy, "that we stoned white kids always want to talk like Negroes?" Lucas was deliberate, paunchy, round-faced, and had a receding hairline—he was well known as a ladies' man. Willy was animated, tall, jumpy, and manically thin—he was well known as an entertaining drunk. And a stoner.

"Negroes! Where?" exclaimed Willy.

They both wore tuxedoes.

"I have learned to restrain myself. It is deeply uncouth to imitate other peoples."

"Ten thousand," countered Willy. "I do believe that's how many of the boogies we took down with our Maxim guns that afternoon."

"Let's take a walk," said Lucas. They left their highballs on the steps of the *Lampoon* castle and meandered down Mount Auburn Street. Everywhere they walked, people shouted hello to them. They were famous across campus for wearing tuxedoes all the time.

Lucas was hungry. "International House of Pancakes," he said.

"Too far to walk, old sport."

"Burritos then. Burritos will make us better men."

Together, they walked into Felipé's, the burrito joint. The walls were painted in Santa Fe adobe colors. Mexican music played from the speakers. Behind the counter were six men and two women, all Hispanic. Lines of students formed at either edge of the counter. Lucas and Willy stepped into line. In front of them was Wilbur the Communist, a well known campus politico.

"What's up, Lucas?" Wilbur greeted them with LA-style hand clasping and back slapping.

"Mexican food," said Lucas, who suddenly realized he was drunker, and higher, than he had thought.

"I hear that, boy," said Wilbur, shifting a bundle of newspapers from one arm to the other.

"Wilbur is a froggy Negro," whispered Willy in Lucas's ear.

Wilbur was short, half white and half Mexican, bald, goateed. He was from Venice Beach, California and he had spent high school skateboarding Oceanfront deck and drinking forties. Eventually he and his friends had come under the spell of a dope-dealing Trotskyist-Leninist named Archie, who wore a white duster over his flowered board shorts. Inspired by Archie, Wilbur had immersed himself in political theory. The Harvard admissions office had been particularly moved by his bid for the Los Angeles City Council Twelfth District seat as a Feuerbachian. He had received over five hundred votes, many of which were from theretofore unregistered voters. Old Jewish folks, gardeners and maids, other skater dudes: he had accompanied them all from the beachwalk to the polling station.

"What are the newspapers, Wilbur?" asked Lucas.

"*Pollo con todo,*" shouted Wilbur over the din. "Ahh, this is a new newspaper by a Boston Leninist cell. BAP. Bo$ton Action Paper. Amateurs, but fuck'em, you know?"

Willy loomed over the guy behind the counter. "Super Chicken," he said, and watched the operation. The guy threw a large soft tortilla on a grill, closed the grill, opened it, and threw the tortilla to the cutting board and a guy standing behind it. This guy asked, "Rice and beans?" and Willy said "Everything," then the guy flung scoops of rice and beans, sour cream, salsa, and guacamole on the tortilla. He rolled it into burrito shape and passed it on to the next guy, who wrapped it in tinfoil and said in Spanish what it was to the woman at the register. She looked at Willy and said "Anything to drink?" and another guy got the lemonade. Like clockwork. It was a joy to be high in there.

"Yo, I always meant to ask you cats a question," said Wilbur, tearing his eyes from Maria, the beautiful register girl, for whom he ate a burrito every day, "why you always wear those tuxedoes?"

"To oppress the masses," said Willy, "to keep the proles down, to crush them under our bespoke heels and maintain the stifling orthodoxies of this ill-conceived experiment in liberty."

Lucas waited tensely for a moment, worried that Willy had gone too far. He had seen Wilbur yelling at people in the yard, following them, arguing. It was something Wilbur was known to do.

"Yo, hah," Wilbur barked, and grabbed his balls in solidarity. "That's a good one, homes."

They were all lucky that everything was so funny.

17

Teak had been working on the Hatashil project for a year before he drove north with the money. Six months before that he had traveled to Kigali. He had two goals for the trip. One was to see the famous silverback gorillas of the Virunga for the Preservation Fund, and the other was to meet an Israeli arms dealer named Marina Levy. She had been selling AK-47s, Hawk antiaircraft missiles, 155 millimeter mortars to Hatashil's young insurgency. Teak was to determine if she had any motives besides profit, and if she didn't, assure her that the United States would let her be. Her small organization had transacted business with the Agency before and she agreed to the meeting knowing why they had asked for it. None of this kept Teak up at night.

In the sunny early afternoon Marina, wearing a crisp white cotton dress covered with small navy polka dots, met Teak at a shaded table by the pool of the Hotel des Milles Collines. She had spent the morning in her bikini at the pool, thinking about religion rather than the meeting because the meeting was only a formality. In Heathrow airport she had picked up a popular book that diagnosed religious faith as an epidemic pathology and the single greatest problem facing humanity. Abused by religion since childhood on a kibbutz near Haifa, she could not agree more, but was troubled by how easy the book was to read and how the arguments were the very ones she might have used when she did her stint in the Israeli Defense Forces nearly a decade before. The author was a famous professor of neuroscience at an Ivy League university and Marina was distressed that she had perhaps attained as sophisticated a loathing of organized religion as she ever would. She had hoped her lack of faith would mature and deepen in complexity, like a good Bordeaux.

Teak was a pleasant surprise for her. He was polite and well-dressed in his khaki suit, not one of the Agency's violent tourists. Usually Marina was the youngest person at meetings but now here was Teak. They each ordered sparkling water.

"Where do you live?" asked Teak.

"Not here."

"Have you seen the gorillas?"

"I really only come here for business," said Marina.

Teak took this as a challenge and described to her their gigantic beauty in the context of the twisting, explosive verdancy of the Virunga. He told her about François, the man who talked with the gorillas, who was already old when Dian Fossey arrived and recognized his talent—although François, of course, had long recognized it in himself. Since François was a small boy he had been unafraid of the gorillas. He had walked close to them, and knew each of them, although he had also been cuffed playfully a few times. He ate the plants to taste what they ate and he knew their smells. And it was partly because of him that Fossey became famous. Teak explained it all with such wonder that after twenty minutes Marina was surprised to find herself attracted to this young man. Even more surprising, she had a small but genuine desire to go and see the gorillas. Over second sparkling waters, they discovered they had a lot in common. Both had been athletes in school. They both had younger siblings. Both liked the same hotel with an old map hanging in the lobby, by the Rodin Museum in Paris, where Marina, in fact, knew the concierge's birthday. She always stayed there, and so did he.

She turned the conversation to work and assured him that she and her people were in it only for the money. He assured her that in that case the United States would leave her alone.

"That's right," she said, "and you must be so busy, fostering freedom around the globe." She was flirting with him.

"Hatashil's good," Teak said.

"Maybe," she said. "But are you good?"

"Where do you vacation," he shot back, "if you only come here for business?"

"Miami."

Teak figured he was obeying orders of some kind when they went to bed that afternoon.

18

The warm fall evening was betrayed by a cold drizzle and David, in a T-shirt and shorts, walked past several homeless men on the street between Adams House and Shay's. One called himself the Champ and shadowboxed in front of the 7-Eleven. David never gave any money to the homeless in Cambridge.

He was looking forward to seeing Jane as he ignored the Champ. He had had a sudden ache for her that afternoon as he sat in the front row of his political economy class. In particular the taste of cigarettes on her lips, which he associated so strongly and stickily with release. He would do anything for her. He couldn't be mad at her about her trip, really. She had supported him, believed in him. She could be flighty and small, he thought, but she wasn't wrong about anything, and she had chosen him. She was definitely on his path.

He knew that much when he started seeing her the spring before, when they spent the days lounging with her friends in front of Holworthy Hall, a freshman dorm. It felt like purposeful lounging, as though not only did Jane and her friends want to laze in Harvard Yard, it was their job. Her friends brought lawn furniture. One, Marvin (whom Jane thought at first she might end up with until he had asked her to suck his dick while they watched a Godard film) brought a kiddie pool several times until it was destroyed. Someone was always playing a guitar and it didn't seem so irritating back then, sometimes it was even sort of pleasant. Sometimes that guy from Stoughton would come and try to play his saxophone but they always managed to stop him by staring at him. The gang in front of Holworthy had formed by that springtime, although they had not yet all slept with each other, had their falling outs. But they had all made it through the first winter together.

When she brought David she could see that look in her girlfriends' eyes. Because he was tall and handsome and African. The dick jokes were made quick and early. But everyone liked him and soon it was first college love. In the warm spring there was nothing either of them wanted more than to sit in the green of Harvard Yard together. His back against a tree, her head in his lap. Feeling the grass under her summer skirt, feeling his fingers in her hair.

As David entered the crowded patio of Shay's he heard Jane's voice like a flute over the top of the bar noise. He was unsurprised to find her holding court at a table of men, including her old suitor, Marvin.

Shay's was Jane's favorite bar because she could smoke there and it was across the street from the Kennedy School of Government and its Institute of Policy. The sunken patio was always packed with a combination of smoking students and locals. It was a prime place for her to run into people she knew.

"No one who isn't from here can really understand the way the place works," Jane was saying.

"You mean here, Harvard?"

"No I mean New York, D.C., wherever. You know, that prep school thing. Money. Growing up with it gives you an understanding. Because if you're rich you can see how the poor live, but if you're poor you can never see how the rich live."

David sat next to her. But he wasn't listening. He was looking across the street, where a cavalcade of black SUVs was parked in defensive formation at the side entrance to the Kennedy School. Jane looked at him and smiled. She always found herself most attracted to him at moments like this, when he seemed to care so little about her friends.

"What's happening over there?" he asked.

Marvin began to explain. "Former ambassador slash congressman Mitchell Harrison, newly appointed intelligence czar. Candidate to watch?" A government major, Marvin wore a mohair blazer over a T-shirt that read "Genghis Tron," and lightly tinted, square glasses. Like many of his peers, he wore his ruthless political ambitions lightly. He spoke in a self-deprecating tenor.

"Future president? I know, I know, I'm totally gay for him, but fighter pilot in Vietnam? Hanoi Hilton?" Marvin went on. "Co-architect of the Afghanistan war with a certain Texas congressman? Intelligence committee? Socially liberal live-free-or-die Democrat?"

"I hate Libertarians," said Jane.

"My idiot sister worked on his campaign," continued Marvin, "which is insane, because now she works at Sotheby's and is getting married, and I'm out of a job. Except hand jobs, which I give myself."

The other boys, his friends and roommates, guffawed or rolled their eyes.

"There's still some Kleenex under your fingernail," said Jane, enjoying Marvin's reflex stare at his right index finger and thumb.

David watched a young woman in a pinstripe suit carry a cardboard box from the back of one of the SUVs to the side entrance. It looked like a heavy box, and the woman was struggling to answer her cell phone as she carried it. David was surprised that the driver standing by the car did not help her.

"Harrison is speaking now?" asked David.

"Fifteen minutes at the IOP in the KSG," said Marvin. He mocked the acronyms tenderly.

"And anyone can go?"

"I would, but look how far away it is," said Marvin, pointing his beer across the street.

Jane read the bored look on David's face and said "Come on. I should go for my story anyway. Maybe he'll talk about Africa." She stubbed her cigarette out, dropped a twenty on the table, and took David by the hand.

As they walked across JFK Street to the Kennedy School of Government, Jane saw about ten protesters: some middle-aged suburban Cantabrigians, some long-haired political Pit kids. They all waved signs decrying the terrorist American government. One was printed with the words "Harrison = Murderer." A bald protestor in a safari vest passed out flyers outlining a world Zionist conspiracy and kept shouting, "I'm a Jew, too!" No one paid any attention to the protesters. A couple of cops in yellow slickers rocked on their heels.

The event was supposed to be ticketed but Jane knew the kid in the bow tie at the door and as he slipped them two tickets he said "we'll quid pro quo someday."

The forum was a multilevel theater, charged with the peculiar mix of celebrity, suspicion, and tired hope that famous politicians bring to college campuses. Photographers from the *Crimson,* the *Independent,* the *Salient,* the *Harvard Political Review,* and *Fifteen Minutes,* equipped with their two-thousand-dollar Nikons checked out from their offices, crowded the press row for a shot of the stage. A potbellied, stubbled *Boston Globe* photographer ignored the press row and knelt in the center aisle. He anticipated making some cash off this, had seen none of his Cambridge beat competition from the *Herald,* and was trying a little harder.

In the center seats were bipartisan members of the Institute of Politics—IOPers, as they were known, boys and girls in blazers who wouldn't object to being called serious young men and women. This was their club, their circus, and they were excited to drink pretentiously cheap beer afterward and talk it over. The Democratic Club and the Republican Club, identical in chinos not jeans, multiethnic, were in their usual spots opposite each other on the second level. Members of the Black Men's Forum, all in sharp suits, sat in a cluster on the third level. Every Friday members wore suits all day. The tradition had existed since the BMF's establishment in 1973. David felt self-conscious in his T-shirt, standing tall in the crowd.

He noticed two secret service guys off to the side of the stage in their dark suits. So different from the NSF, he thought. The NSF liked their uniforms. The more badges and medals the better. In contrast, the only badges David saw in the forum were the flag pins on the lapels of the young Republicans.

"I wonder if we'll get any wackos tonight," David heard one of the IOPers say.

Jane pointed toward the stage. "Look, your professor girlfriend."

Susan Lowell sat in the second row, the only woman. On her left was Razi, notebook on his lap.

History Chair Henry Rose introduced Director Harrison as an old friend first—they had met at Yale—and then as a patriot and legendary diplomat. Polite applause as Harrison took the stage.

Susan leaned to Razi's ear. "I didn't realize they were such old friends."

"They grew up together in the same building on Fifth Avenue." Razi looked at her eyelashes in profile as he spoke into her ear, "They used to race their chauffeurs to school at St. Bernard's."

Director Harrison was bald, his square face gray and mottled by liver spots. He walked to the podium with a slight limp. The American flag pin on his slim-cut suit caught the light. He would deliver this particular speech from notecards. As he began he caught the eye of a tall young African and though he was not superstitious he considered it slightly unsettling.

The speech was specifically about David's part of the world. Director Harrison said reports of human rights violations had been legitimate, but in his opinion and the opinion of the intelligence community, the Al-Kateb government of Somalia was taking serious steps toward reform and a stabilizing influence. The National Security Front was not a criminal organization. And in his opinion, yes, this was an example of the media sensationalizing an issue to the detriment of all parties concerned.

The crowd grew murmurous with the realization that Harrison was saying something new. The IOPers were excited to be on hand for a speech that would surely make national news the next day. Harrison went on to describe the NSF as a key ally in the War on Terror. And that all should be reminded by *Hatashil's Massacre,* that we must place our trust in stable government, rather than vigilantes and self-styled liberators who capitalize on disorder. He ended by calling what he had just said a disappointing truth.

"This is the exact opposite," said Jane to David, "of what every media organization and NGO is reporting. How can he say this?" She scribbled question marks in her moleskin notebook. David felt the peculiar sensation that comes from watching a powerful man tell lies.

Susan Lowell and Razi exchanged puzzled looks. The one laudable foreign policy of the administration so far was being tough on Al-Kateb. And now a reversal.

"He just coined it. Be on Wikipedia tomorrow," said Razi.

"What?" asked Susan. But she knew. She just didn't know why she wasn't angrier.

Hatashil's Massacre.

19

Predawn. Teak signaled as he turned back onto the main track. He realized as he did this that it was a crazy thing to do. There was nothing but scrub in any direction. Maybe somewhere miles off in a tree a *shifta* with a lifted pair of tourist Nikons saw the signal. *Maybe those dead village kids were living in the trees now, strange acacia spirits, noting his signal. Maybe those paramilitaries, whoever they were, were drinking St. George lager in Addis.*

It was a bad drive already. Before he left the village he had debriefed his superior, Lunt, by scrambled cell phone. Lunt had sounded funny, clicked off fast to try to get satellite going. Said he would call back but hadn't. So Teak was driving back to Nairobi. His mind raced, then emptied. Then raced again. As though the aerial ordinance had shaken some dark water loose in his brain. Every villager had tried to fight, their guns appearing from nowhere. But they never stood a chance. And then they were bodies on the ground.

It's hard but I like it.

Because Teak was thinking and not driving carefully, the Land Cruiser lurched sideways and caught abruptly in a narrow ditch. He got out to inspect and remembered driving around the ditch on the trip in. *Careless*. The dawn broke then and the track became very hot. He would have to rock his way out, reverse and turn the wheel just so. And like a mosquito by his ear, banished but not forgotten, the thought that it had been an American operation.

Reverse, shift, forward, reverse, easing out of the ditch. The sun rose higher and the dust on the track seemed to Teak to rise almost like steam. Reverse, shift, forward, reverse, easing out of the ditch. The damn Land Cruiser wouldn't come out of the ditch. Teak mentally scolded himself for not focusing. He killed the engine and stared through the windshield down the hot empty track. He opened the glove box and took out the Harvard mug from the village and turned it over in his hands.

The shard of Fanta can, thought Teak, the almost knife. *Execution or escape*. That damn Fanta kid was getting under his skin. He wondered if he would have fought like that when he was thirteen.

Teak got out and stood in the track to stretch his legs and clear his head. He knew he would get the car out eventually. He looked down at his shoes in the dirt. He had never felt guilty before and he didn't know why he did now. It wasn't his fault.

His phone rang.

"Hello?"

"Go to the airstrip at Naivasha," said Lunt. "There'll be a plane waiting for you."

The line went dead.

20

After the speech Jane and David walked upstairs so she could check her e-mail at one of the communal computers. She didn't have a blackberry on principle. They stopped for a moment on the mezzanine. Below them, on the ground floor, Director Harrison shook one hand after another, the party in orbit around him. Jane picked out an ambitious news reporter from the *Crimson* waiting for an opening to ask a question. Good, she thought, I can use his notes.

As they continued up to the third floor, they encountered an extremely dour Wilbur. He was frowning and shaking his head, leaning over the balcony. Jane put her hand on his shiny scalp and rubbed it as if for good luck.

"Hey, homes," she said, imitating him, "wassup."

"When they lock our asses up, when you keep hearing that click-click on the phone," he answered, "that's when all these people, *inshallah,* will wish they had done something besides sell Facebook to the State Department."

"Are you actually that mad about this?" asked Jane.

"Fuck you," said Wilbur.

"Hey," interceded David.

"And your indy cred," Wilbur concluded, flipping his hood up. He shoved his hands in his pockets and walked off.

"What's indy cred?"

Jane looked at David and rolled her eyes. "Jeez. He's probably headed to his dorm room to catch up on the reading for cosmic connections."

As Jane checked her e-mail, David thought about why Director Harrison had said what he did. The American media did not cover the story every day and they got it wrong anyway, but most of Harvard knew that the NSF was basically made up of war criminals. Their administration was crippled by infighting, the various factions sucked all oil and resources into themselves along the half dozen paved roads—and when the peripheries demanded their share, one faction or another killed them. Called them *zirga, niggers, slaves,* let them starve. Or turned them against each other. This incoherent greedy madness was what Hatashil was fighting, region wide, and what Susan Lowell's book exposed. The NSF had become the focus of a kind of idealistic rage, even for people who knew little. David was proud that his father had sewn up one of Hatashil's rebels, and proud that America was on his father's side and denounced the actions of the NSF. Some even called it genocide. It wasn't quite like that, thought David, but it could be. So why would America change its mind?

"I got into the conference," Jane said, tapping the screen happily. "I'm going to Kenya." She wrapped her arms around him and kissed him on the cheek.

As if you weren't going anyway. David didn't say anything. He was happy for her, he guessed, happy that she was justifying her vacation somehow. David hated school vacations. For him, the cheapest plane ticket cost to much, and that was with a sixteen-hour layover in Heathrow. His father had helped and David had saved money from dorm crew so he had gone home for part of the summer. But he couldn't afford to go back more than once a year. He would spend a strange Christmas with the other foreigners in Harvard's empty houses. He clung to the memory of his month at home.

"Now I just have to do this story before I leave." Jane started running some more ideas about Hatashil and Lowell at David, but he wasn't really listening.

He had returned a hero. He spent his time with his father, making rounds with him in the ancient pickup that served as a mobile clinic. As a veterinarian David's father was highly esteemed. Especially now that his son went to Harvard, though that name meant less than simply *the United States*. With David home to help, his father resolved to work twice as hard and to visit his most remote clients. These most remote clients were actually some of his favorites, and David's, too. It was not always profitable to make the trip—compensation was usually in goat—but David's father made it when he could. And after all, some of the clients were family.

David's great grandfather had moved from country to town as a young boy, to work for the *wazungu* to survive. It was the 1890s, years of recurring drought. The rinderpest had killed nearly every cow and the world coffee market had crashed. Then the smallpox epidemic of 1899. But he had run the house for an especially generous *mzungu* and eventually used the money he saved to buy a large *shamba,* or tract of land. In 1925, when the African Native Reserves had been officialized, he shrewdly flipped his plot, realizing that real estate was more profitable than agriculture in the soon to be overpopulated reserves. He had kept trading, flipping, and trading up, until his son, David's grandfather, could go to the capital and learn veterinary medicine. This cemented the family's place in the small native middle class.

David's great-granduncle, however, had remained in the country. His line was still there, living in a village and these were the remote clients. David's father was more than happy to pull the most insidious worms from his cousin's cows and goats, sit in on their councils as an honored guest, drink *pombe*. And, of course, the cousins knew the fighting in the bush, and sometimes sheltered warriors. David's father didn't want to know too much, in case he ever had a problem with the NSF in town. But he had once arrived at the same time as some of Hatashil's men and dug a bullet out of a man's leg.

"Consider the prophecy of Syokimau," said David's father as they drove north toward the cousins' village. "'I see men coming on the water . . . they will start laying a long snake across the country . . .' Isn't that something?"

It was difficult to get books but his father liked to ramble about whatever he had last read. David was ever the obedient son, and even in his favored position as returning Harvard student he was extremely polite and respectful. His father was old.

"You may think it is foolish to visit our cousins but in fact it is very important. The rest of the prophecy continues, 'These are strange people, so white that one can almost see their intestines. When they settle in our country they will spoil it first by forcing us to divide it up amongst ourselves.'"

David thought of Widener Library at Harvard, as he wondered where his father had found such a lunatic quote. A core class would tear that quote apart. Where did it come from? What was the purpose, whose propaganda? Where was the money? David felt as though he could not explain any of this to his father. He had known when he left for Boston that he would see things that his father would never see, but he had not known the change so acutely until that moment. It surprised him.

They parked along the stream by the date palm. David unslung his Eastpak bag from his shoulder as the children ran to greet him, beloved visitor, cousin David. From the bag, he handed out a half dozen Harvard mugs. Toys you could use. David's father kept one of the mugs for himself, and putting his hand on David's shoulder, said, "It is good to visit our cousins, don't you agree with me?"

"I wish you could come with me," said Jane. "It would be so great for you to show me around. Then I could really understand the place."

"Yes," said David, and imagined introducing Jane to his father.

21

Teak's first time in Africa.

He went on safari with his family and one other family, the Greens. The two families vacationed together frequently. Alan Green, his father's friend, had three daughters. Teak had two brothers. Teak and his brothers went to Buckley and Exeter, the Green girls went to Brearley. They were all about the same age. Teak thought all the Green girls were pretty and felt graceless around them, though at various times they all secretly adored him.

The safari was as expensive as it could be, and Teak's father paid for it all. He was a surgeon and had patented a part of a pacemaker. Each tent had two *boys*. Each *boy* was responsible for one guest, for putting a hot water bottle in the guest's bed each night and waking the guest with hard sweet biscuits and coffee or tea on a silver tray in the morning. And any other tasks. Teak felt the injustice of service acutely—the constitution of a world that arbitrarily provided one man to *serve* another. The *boys* made him uneasy. Being a *boy* was considered a good job.

Like all men the *boys* had some loves and vengeances and so on lodged in their hearts, but no pacemakers, and there never would be. They expect you to give them things to do, the guide told Teak and his family, wouldn't understand if they weren't told what to do.

Before dawn one morning, the guests were driven over the winding pitted tracks of the Masai Mara to a hot air balloon. It was July and the wildebeests were migrating. It is the largest migration of biomass in the world, one of the khaki guides had told Teak. Coming over a hill in the darkness, the Land Cruiser's lights had suddenly flashed in the eyes of thousands of wildebeests. Teak thought that it looked like the window lights of the New York skyline, but he kept this thought to himself. Teak had tried, at sixteen, always to say less than he was thinking.

At the hot air balloon launch Teak's family and the Greens all slid into the same basket, which could carry a dozen passengers. Around them, a team of Africans in red jumpsuits busily arranged ropes and gunned heavy fans into the balloon. Teak had no idea where the jumpsuit men were from or who they were but he wanted to know. None of his family or friends seemed to be paying much attention to these men. Even though these Africans were about to launch them to the heavens.

When the balloon was three-quarters full, the Belgian balloonist in knee socks and shorts set up the great silver torch and pulled a lever. Yellow flames roared into the air over the basket and Teak felt the heat, slightly, on his face.

The wind gusted suddenly and they all heard a sharp pop. Then the balloon was sliding fast across the savannah toward the half dozen parked Land Cruisers. The anchor line had snapped. Teak's father yelled for everyone to keep their arms in the basket. He had a quick vision of one of the children trying to get out and snapping a tibia or humerus between the basket and the ground. The Belgian cursed and yelled at the red-jumpsuited staff running after the basket, clinging to loose ropes. Some of the jumpsuits simply stood dumbly, watching. One of the Green girls screamed. The Belgian struggled with the clips that fastened the basket to the balloon. They would smash into the cars in moments.

And then Alan Green, who was not as fit as he once was, swore in Greek and jumped nimbly to the edge of the basket and unclipped what the Belgian could not. And as quickly as the slide began it stopped, and the basket settled in the risen dust, and the deflating, detached balloon plastered itself over the Land Cruisers. The Belgian apologized profusely and looked at Green with wonder.

That night Teak had his first conversation with Alan Green about languages. They had been sitting around the campfire in foldout canvas chairs before a dinner of steak flown in from Nairobi. Teak was studying Arabic at Exeter. He had studied Latin since fourth grade and French since fifth.

"How's the Arabic going?" asked Green in the flicker of the fire. A boy brought him a Bombay Sapphire and Krest tonic on a tray.

"It's hard but I like it," said Teak. This was his answer to everything when he was sixteen. Across the campfire, one of the guides, a former employee of Shell in West Africa, was regaling the Green girls and Teak's two brothers with a story.

"And then I looked over," Teak heard the guide's Sussex accent, "and I saw a Chinese man sawing the head off a dog . . ."

Teak listened to his brothers laugh.

"Do you ever think about studying *these* languages?" asked Green.

"You mean like Swahili? They don't offer them at Exeter."

"I mean in college. Swahili, Somali, Lingala for the Congo. There's a lot of sharing between Arabic and the East African languages."

"I'll think about it," said Teak.

"That's what I might learn, if I was going to school now. I was just thinking about it, as I watched the balloon guys in the jumpsuits today. I was wondering where they were from," said Green.

Every time Teak talked with Alan Green he wanted to be closer to him, to have some kind of bond beyond his father. He kept silent, not sure what to say. And then, "Mr. Alan, Mr. Mike," one of the boys startled him. "Now is the time to eat."

PART II

Garissa, Kenya, 200X

"Are you scared of all theses whites?" David's father asks him when they first enroll him at the colonial school.

David shakes his head.

"These ones here, they are fine people," says his father.

22

The airstrip was a hundred yards of packed dirt on the plains. Standing at it's terminus, wishing for shade, Teak looked out over a clear mile to a black burned stain of earth, ignited by lightening and since extinguished by time and space. As Teak noticed a hyena trotting along in the distance, dull gold against the black, his phone rang again.

"You've got new orders. We've changed your assignment," Lunt said. "First you'll be debriefed. I'll be in touch." He coughed thickly into the phone, and finishing, told Teak to enjoy the beach.

"What's this about Hatashil hitting his own people?" asked Teak, "that's not what happened."

Lunt hung up on him again. Teak didn't want to get on the plane to some safe house. He wanted to go to Lunt's office at the embassy. If he explained what had happened they could sort this out. They couldn't lie about it if he had been right there on the ground. It must be a fuck-up. *Incompetent, not evil,* he tried to remind himself. But he couldn't just go in and fix it. Lunt said get on the plane, and Teak didn't disobey orders.

* * *

The Cessna cruised noisily over the Indian Ocean. Teak glanced at the pilot and then looked down at the plane's shimmering reflection in the water. The pilot didn't know anything except the destination.

Teak had been surprised at Lunt's abruptness. The culture in the Agency was pretentious bureaucracy, but Lunt was usually forthright. He never killed the phone like this. He never issued *orders*.

Teak had not felt the full force of the hierarchy since training. And even then he had been immune from its sting, Alan Green's godson, crack shot, young at the top of the class, immediately stationed. He knew he was valuable. He operated as one of only a half dozen nonofficial covers, or NOLs, in the region. He was the only officer fluent in all the local languages *not that anyone gave a shit about those languages*. Working with the East Africa Wildlife Preservation Fund, Teak liasoned for visiting patrons, recorded the decline of the crested cranes with scientists, sympathized with poachers. He was friends with a clique of biology grad students—reasonable, young, some Muslims, who were themselves nervy about the NSF, and knew that elements in Khartoum were running elements in Mogadishu but had no notion what Teak's real job was. Everyone hoped for more bird-watchers one day but Teak knew that the NSF was increasingly aggressive and militant and that there would be less bird-watching before more.

There in the plane, Teak felt like he was being sent home from school, or to detention. In high school, he received his single detention for failing to hand in a paper on Aristotle. The reading had seemed so ancient and backward that he had left the paper to the last moment and then forgotten about it. In the end he studied Aristotle's universe very hard, because he had hated being punished. Flying now, he imagined himself somewhere in the middle of that universe. So above Teak, the moon, the stars, the sun, God. Below him, in degenerating circles of uncleanliness, God's creatures, man, and beneath his feet, Earth, and then Hades. *And that damn kid with the Fanta can*. Ahead of him a low ridge of billowing cumulus clouds hovered above a small, thickly green archipelago. *Who knew that purgatory would look so fine?*

Three men waited to greet Teak at the end of the short grass runway. The air was humid. A hand-sized black lacewing buzzed Teak's ear as he disembarked. He could smell the ocean even though the runway was in the middle of the island. One of the men, compact and olive-skinned beneath a fine blue linen shirt, stuck out a hand. "Welcome to Funzi," he said, taking off his Panama hat. "I am Francisco."

Francisco spoke with a complicated accent, a slight Basque lisp attenuating his *s*es. The other men were African, and silent, and no introductions were made. One took Teak's bag and carried it to the truck waiting nearby.

"Mr. Lunt has arranged for everything," said Francisco. "If there is anything at all we can do for you while you are here, please you just ask me. The philosophy is that this is a home."

Teak was surprised. Lunt operated under official cover at the embassy, was careful not to associate himself directly with any of the NOCs. And clearly, this guy Francisco knew they were connected. One of the African guys started the truck and they began a bumpy drive through the hanging creepers and sun-drenched bromeliads. Francisco continued warmly, "You should be completely comfortable. Set your own meal times and eat what you like. We have five cuisines available: Italian, French, Szechuan, there is a Tokyo-trained sushi chef, and what I think is the best, the local Swahili coast cuisine, which is mostly seafood, of course."

Teak blinked as the jungle thinned out for a hundred yards and they drove by a cleared field. In the corner of the field he could see a three-walled building and a number of children sitting before a blackboard in its shade. A teacher tapped the board for their attention as every head swiveled at the sound of the truck.

"If you care for fishing or water sport," Francisco was saying, "we have some sailboats and windsurfers and so on. George the boatman can help you. Also there is a our little spa," he motioned at a shingled wigwam structure as they passed. "Ursula is new, but she is an extremely talented masseuse."

Teak inhaled deeply. The smell of the ocean was very strong now. As they rounded a final turn, a white stone building rose above them under a high *makuti* thatched roof. Beyond it Teak could see the white sand beach and the steady lap of the Indian Ocean. The truck stopped. Teak heard children laughing somewhere. From around the corner of the building, a white girl peeked at him. Her hair was cut like a schoolboy's, and her head seemed crooked on her neck. Her staring eyes bulged slightly, and then she was gone.

Francisco turned to Teak and looked directly into his eyes. "Or, of course," he said, "you can do nothing at all and we will stay absolutely out of your way. Many come here purely for privacy."

* * *

Francisco settled him into his *banda* and expressed his hope that Teak would join him and his wife for dinner, if he was so inclined. And then Teak was alone again. He stripped to his shorts and stepped outside to scout. His *banda* was on an inlet, down the beach from the main building where they had parked. The strange girl was on the beach, staring at him for a moment but taking off when he came outside, ignoring his wave. Down the beach there were only ten *banda*s and at the moment only one other seemed occupied. Teak recognized an American movie actress and her British rock-star husband lounging on their veranda. The beach was quiet. Francisco was nowhere to be seen.

By a line of Lasers and small catamarans, a calloused African introduced himself as George the boatman and asked Teak if he wanted to sail. Teak declined. Continuing around the compound, he saw a blonde he presumed to be Ursula, topless on a towel, reading a coverless paperback. Soon there was nothing left to scout. Nothing to do. *That's why I'm here,* he thought. *To stop thinking. Not so easy*. He walked down to the water.

The ocean felt like a warm bath. Teak floated on his back and blinded himself staring up into the sky. His mind slowed and wandered. First to the strange girl who had stared at him, twice, so intently. Then his mind went to the Fanta kid, even though he tried to think of other things.

That night Francisco, his wife Claudia, the famous couple, and Teak sat at a round table under the high roof of the white store building and felt the sea breeze as they ate. Claudia was perhaps thirty years younger than Francisco, ink haired and tanned to the color of dark sand. She was just showing pregnant. As he sat down, Teak felt an unusual pang of loneliness.

On Francisco's recommendation they all decided on Swahili lobster, which came cracked on a bed of rice with bright mango salsa. After they talked about the food, they talked about education. The movie actress asked about the school she had seen on the way in. Francisco had built it for the children on the island, but it was just a start. He planned on several buildings, with air conditioning. "My older children are grown and gone," he explained. "School in England. But by the time this one is ready," he patted Claudia's small belly, "maybe I poach a teacher from Eton for a year."

There were about five hundred people on the island. Before Francisco had acquired the land and its central building—from the son of a navy minister, who needed to raise money for a parliamentary bid—the inhabitants had almost entirely been illiterate fishermen. Now about a hundred of them worked for him. The hotel had started as his beach home, but he loved the place and realized that the way to have interesting houseguests was to turn it into a hotel. It worked by word of mouth. Francisco didn't advertise. Teak wondered how often it served as a safe house, and for whom.

Black hands wrapped around the necks of the wine bottles and the bottles disappeared and reappeared. Teak was a good drinker and so was Francisco. The famous couple just sipped at the beginning but then the husband got drunk. The sun set red and quickly.

"It's a secret, but I'll tell all of you," said the movie actress. "We're pregnant, too!"

Champagne!

The movie actress, who already seemed to count Claudia as a dear friend, said that was why she had been thinking about schools. She had attended private school in New York, like Teak—she was only a little older, they knew people in common. And she thought maybe she ought to raise her child out of all of that madness. Francisco agreed. He said he hadn't been to New York in twenty years and didn't miss it. Though, of course, the schools were among the best in the world.

The conversation was interrupted by the arrival of the strange girl, and Teak saw she was no girl but a woman, close in age to himself. She was heavy, carried wide hips in unflattering jeans, and large pendulous breasts beneath an oversized gray T-shirt. She approached the table smiling shyly, and then tried to hide behind Francisco.

"Maria," he said, "we have guests."

Teak saw her peeking at him from behind Francisco's shoulder.

"This is my daughter, Maria," he said. Maria removed her head from his shoulder and smiled a toothy, crooked smile. The actress and rock star smiled and waved at her but she did not take her eyes off Teak.

"Hello, Maria," said Teak, standing up and bowing slightly as he said it.

Maria blushed and walked over to the railing at the edge of the dining hall. She ran her fingers along it and looked out at the sea, glancing back at the table every few moments.

"Anyone for desert or coffee?" asked Claudia.

"Suppose another wine instead," said Francisco. In the years following Maria's birth he had amassed a formidable cellar.

There had been nights when he looked at the pregnant clouds over the Indian Ocean and drank with the conviction that a bottle of wine was the first and only true unit of measure in an evil universe. He thought if he drank enough maybe he would soak his brain into the moody animal indifference that Maria had been born with. He forgave himself those young father's thoughts, though not for several years.

"Your daughter is sweet," said Teak.

23

Razi made a pact with himself not to get drunk at Susan's Pulitzer party. But he decided to have a drink before he went. He took his beer out to the front stoop of his apartment building to enjoy the fall afternoon. He had meant to call a friend at Reuters about the Hatashil thing, but he hadn't. He'd napped. Clouds were blowing in from the east and Razi guessed there would be rain soon. He watched the leaves blow across the street.

When he finished his beer and turned back inside he was surprised to see something in his mailbox. He had not received a single piece of mail aside from university paperwork since he had moved in. Now there was an unmarked padded envelope. Inside, he found a CD and nothing else. At his desk, Razi turned on his computer for the first time that day and inserted the CD, somehow knocking over a full ashtray in the process. Ashes all over the keyboard. *Fuck*. He'd get it later.

The disc was bad news. The screen went black. First the Harvard logo, then Susan's face appeared and her voice came, tinny, out of his speakers. As she spoke, the picture changed, turning into a dead child, a burning village, open bodies.

"No one in the whole Horn hears or sees anything. What's thirty lives in a war? Give a shit if thirty Africans are killed? I'd kill that many people with my bare hands."

Her face and name, and beneath that "Harvard University" appeared again after the last line was uttered.

"Fuck," said Razi. It was her voice, he couldn't help but recognize it. *She always did have a temper,* he thought. But this was something else.

Emily Lowell, age seven, heard the front door buzzer and raced down the stairs.

"Who is it?" she said through the door.

"Razi," said Razi.

"How do I know?"

"Suppose I know your birthday?"

"No you don't."

"May second?"

"That's my brother's birthday!"

Outside in the rain, Razi thought he was not such a bad godfather at all.

"Suppose I know your whole name . . . Emily Isabelle Lowell?"

The girl opened the door. Razi scooped her up squealing and carried her to the kitchen. Ellie, the housekeeper, stood at the stove stirring a pot of pasta, talking on a portable phone. "Okay, bye," said Ellie and put the phone down. Her friends and relatives and the various Jamals were accustomed to her quick hang ups. At her feet, Jamal Jr. played with a handheld gaming device. At the kitchen table, four-year-old Ford Lowell watched Jamal with open suspicion and hostility.

"Hello, Ellie," said Razi.

"Uh, hi," said Ellie.

"Can I measure you?" Emily asked Razi. She took a tailor's small tape measure from her pocket and drew it up along Razi's leg to his hip, where it ran out.

"You are much taller than I first suspected," she said.

Susan Lowell, wrapped in a towel, with another around her hair, walked into the kitchen and picked her BlackBerry up off the counter, greeting Razi as if she were fully clothed.

"Hi," Razi said, flushing. *For fuck's sake,* he thought, he'd seen her weep and skinny dip, he didn't know why he was embarassed now. He fingered the disc in his pocket. He was not looking forward to playing it for her. He had considered waiting until after the party but that would be against their rules. She'd want to know.

"Mommy," said Ford, "Jamal took my PlayStation."

"Let him play with it for a while," said Susan, walking to her bedroom. "I'll be right out."

Razi sat next to the pouting Ford, who seemed to be picking up on his anxiety. The child stared at him, dogfaced.

"It's a big night for your mom," Razi said. "Everyone is coming out to congratulate her at school."

This did not cheer Ford up.

"We had cupcakes at my school on my birthday," said Emily.

Razi took his Zippo from his pocket. "Here," he said, showing Ford. "This is better than a PlayStation." Razi showed Ford how to use it. Emily crowded them. The phone rang and Ellie answered it and began talking rapidly in high pidgin.

Upstairs, Susan was frowning into her closet. She could not decide. It was only at these goddamn academic cocktail parties that she ever had this dilemma. The problem was that she had too much to wear. She should have just the one black suit, *ha ha,* but she had more than a dozen in various shades of navy and black. Shopping was one of the things she and Harry did together. He was going to meet her at the party later. It was extravagant and fun for both of them. Matte black, she decided, and in another minute sat on the edge of her bed putting on her heels. Razi knocked on the door and stepped into the room.

"You look good," he said.

"Some of these people would step on the back of my head as soon as say hello."

They looked at each other across the rich, untidy bedroom, Razi trying to read Susan's surprised expression. *What are you doing in my bedroom?*

"Where's your laptop?" He asked. "I need to show you something."

It was in her oversized purse on the floor and she plugged it in and they sat on her bed and watched.

"What the fuck," said Susan when it was over. "No demand with it?"

"Did you say all that?"

She tried to remember, looked at her face staring out at her from the screen. It was the same screen at which she had written the book, at which she had lived her life for the last five years. *What did it matter?* She knew she should be furious, should be torching contacts. But all she felt was the absence of that anger.

"Lunt," she remembered aloud. "That was where it came from. I said those things, but not like that."

"It's a threat," said Razi.

"Let's go to the party," she sighed, and then, for Razi's benefit, "We'll figure it out."

As he followed her down the stairs Razi almost laughed. Weird as this shit was, it was nice to be back with her, it felt like they were working again. He stood to the side as she said good-bye to Ford and Emily as if nothing had happened.

"Okay, kiddos," said Susan, kissing each of her children. "Be good. I'll see you in the morning."

"Where are you going?" asked Emily.

"Oh, Em, I've told you a thousand times, there's a party because I won that prize."

"Don't go," said Ford, his face like an ice cube about to crack under hot water.

"I have to go, sweetie," Susan told him as she and Razi made for the front door. "I'll check in on you when I get home."

Ford wailed. Jamal Jr. looked up briefly from his game and then back down into it. Ellie cast a "you shittin' me" glance over her shoulder at no one in particular. Ford cried at high pitch and followed Susan and Razi to the front door. Susan knelt down and comforted her son but he would not stop screaming. He demanded that she not leave. Emily followed and joined the argument.

“Ellie,” called Susan, “come here and help, please?”

Ford grabbed onto Susan’s leg, preventing her from walking out the door. Emily did the same to Razi, more playfully but also screaming now. Jamal followed his mother to the front hall and now stood, staring at the scene, holding the PlayStation in both hands. Susan finally knelt and with Ellie’s help pried Ford off her leg.

“Jamal,” barked Ellie. “Give da ting here,” and she held out her hand for the PlayStation. Jamal gave it to her, and this was the last thing Razi saw before Susan had closed the door behind them and they were walking down Acorn Street into the rainy, cobbled Beacon Hill evening.

In the cab, Razi offered her a sip from his flask.

“I am a bad mother,” Susan said, tapping the window.

“Your mum and dad, they fuck you up,” said Razi, taking an extra sip for her since she had declined.

“Larkin didn’t have to breast feed during tenure review.”

“The CD means they’re here. It was delivered by hand, not mailed.”

“Not the first threat,” she said.

“But Cambridge, not Khartoum.”

“Well, whoever they are. I don’t really care, Razi.”

She always was tough, thought Razi. He looked at her in the rainy taxi window light. It made her skin soft, like a shell underwater. Softer, or maybe just younger. For a while, following Toma around together almost blindly, they had done everything together except have sex. On the nights when they had to share a room in some flea-blasted, bandit town he drank a lot of whatever was around but still did not hit on her. He wondered if it had ever crossed her mind. It must have. He considered himself a brave man, except that he had never made a pass at her. Or maybe he had. Razi suspected that he had tried to kiss her when he was drunk and she remembered and held it over him in some way. But really, he thought, he knew the problems. He was shorter than she was, and maybe a drunk, and would never really have any money. This was strange for a Persian of his class, as was clear every time his cousins showed off their jewelry at a social event in New York or Los Angeles. But some families, like his, hadn't invested right, didn't get enough out when it mattered. All he really had was an education, which would have served him well as a banker or doctor. But he wasn't a banker or doctor, he was a journalist. This and the Al-Emudi story—the foundation his success, his fame as an Iranian journalist, *well sourced from the Gulf to the Horn*. He knew he was handsome, but not right for her. He never got that exactly. Except he did. *Racism everywhere*.

By the time the opportunity to interview Hatashil came, Razi was in love with her. They had been on the story together, on and off, for years. Except she wasn't on a story, she was researching her dissertation. And then only one of them could go. Only one seat on the plane and all that, theatrics on the dirt runway. Toma could not stop rolling his eyes. Razi supposed he gave her the spot out of love, but also he knew that he wasn't going to write a book, do the work. The interview would improve his reputation, but what would it be? Five thousand words of action politics in the *Atlantic*. Razi had hoped that she would do something better with it. And here they were, six years later, on the way to the Pulitzer celebration.

When she had thanked him it was not by falling into bed with him.

And then she had returned to London and met Harry.

When she suggested that Razi apply for the Nieman Fellowship for a year he wanted to say no, but then he applied.

Susan Lowell was still staring out the window.

"Excuse me," Razi said to the driver, "can I smoke in here?"

24

Teak stood at the ultramarine water. *I'm not here on vacation,* he thought. *They must want me to think. Or do something else.* He didn't know, and he didn't like not knowing. *If I am here to think, then I'll think about the Hatashil project.* Every morning he sat in the hot sand, looking at the ocean, and recalled other mornings. From the beginning.

A stone room eleven months ago, where Teak had already waited two days for his contact, where the fuzz of a radio floated up to his ears and brought him to consciousness. He rose nude and leaned out the window, looking over the boatyard, alive with enterprise, and the shipping containers, and fecal garbage, out to the sea. The rough stone of the windowsill left its texture on his forearms. There were a couple of kids playing football at the shore, and some goats nosing around in the trash.

"Good morning," said a voice behind him. His gun was on the other side of the room.

"Good morning," said Teak, turning carefully. He faced a coffee-skinned man who was wearing gold-rimmed glasses on his aquiline nose, and a white polo shirt.

The man's cell phone rang to the tune of "(I Can't Get No) Satisfaction."

"Excuse me," he said, and answered it.

Teak dressed quickly in his khaki suit as he watched his visitor listen with the phone to his ear.

"*Shukran,*" said the visitor finally, and hung up. How at ease this man was, thought Teak, having just let himself into another man's room. Like he was in charge.

"I'm Toma," the man said and extended a hand. They shook but Teak did not introduce himself.

"Sorry to barge in," said Toma, handing Teak a photograph. "This is a few years old?"

Teak looked at the black-and-white image of himself staring blankly into the camera, taken his freshman year. "University ID photo," said Teak, "Mind if I get dressed?"

"Fortunately, you seem to be who you are," said Toma. "So. Sorry I'm late, you know how it goes. Stuck outside of Mobile with the Memphis blues again. The car is downstairs." Teak and Toma did not trust each other but that was part of their jobs.

Leaving town, they slowed to a stop for a herd of cattle crossing the road and it seemed to Teak that the cowbells complemented the idling of the engine.

"You studied languages at university," said Toma.

"I did."

"You do not talk very much for someone who studies languages."

"What do you want to talk about?" asked Teak, watching a child bring his switch down on a small cow.

"Proverbs," said Toma.

"*Furahi ya nyanyi huisha jangwani*," said Teak.

"Very nice. The happiness of the monkey does indeed end in the desert. I like 'it ain't me, I ain't no fortunate son,'" Toma said, studying Teak as he said it.

"That's not a proverb, " Teak said.

The small cow stopped in the middle of the road. The child brought the switch down repeatedly on the cow's hindquarters. "He's not doing it right," Toma said, jabbing a finger at the boy in the road.

Toma got out of the car and took the switch from the boy. Teak couldn't hear what was said but Toma hit the troublesome cow in a way the boy hadn't and the herd moved across the road. Then Toma leaned over and put the switch back in the boy's hand and showed him how to do it. Teak liked him better for this.

The valley had been a popular hideout since before spears were guns and that day it was hazy and visibility was bad. In the afternoon they came to the ridge. At its base a faded Italian colonial building rose incongruously against the wild scrub. They had been driving for a hundred miles on bad road.

"There was man named Kennedy who used to lived here," said Toma, as they walked around the building to a makeshift corral. There were discarded tires on the ground inside the enclosure. *Fucked up,* thought Teak as the horses stepped around them. *Always fucked up.*

"Kennedy is a strange name for around here," volunteered Teak.

"Named for the greatest American king," Toma snorted derisively. "Parents valued education, read Italian. Anyway. He left. Some affair with an Italian aid worker."

"Where'd he go?" asked Teak.

"Nairobi. Who knows. Hey," Toma said to the boy who was now helping him saddle up, "you know where Kennedy went?"

"No," said the boy brightly. He had never seen a white person this close before, and he was excited by Teak. He was proud that Toma, whom he had saddled up several times before, was asking him questions in front of the stranger. He puffed out his chest at Teak. Teak recalled the boys on his high school safari. For his part, Toma was relieved that Teak could ride. Not all Americans could. In spite of television. Not that there was anything to it.

Teak learned to ride because Alan Green, Teak's godfather, was from a ranching family. Green was thus an oddity at Harvard in his time there, but still made a fast, almost vertical ascent through the culture of the college and, ultimately, the Agency. Green rarely took time off but once, when he did, he invited Teak's family out to the Union Ranch. A quarter of a million acres in New Mexico.

Teak and Green grew closer on that trip to New Mexico. And Teak's father encouraged the kinship between his son and his friend, though he never imagined where it would lead. He was a clever doctor and especially skillful in the operating room, but not good on a horse. His best friend, Alan Green, rode well, had an investment in the crude physical world outside of clean rooms and the valves of the heart. Teak was always drawn to this, and his father knew it.

Green essentially taught the boy how to ride on that trip. Teak was a natural but impatient. One particular afternoon he harped on galloping. He and the other children had been allowed to walk, trot, canter, but not gallop. In what became an often told story in both families, Teak, in child's Stetson, ignoring his parents, galloped off, couldn't hold on, and was thrown from his horse.

Green raced to him, frightened, frustrated that he had not stopped the boy as he took off. The early fears of parenthood had long dissipated, but kneeling by Teak they returned, the feeling that the child was as soft as clay, hollow, filled with jam. Green imagined a forehead stoved in with by a hoof.

One of the wranglers rode up with Teak's small Stetson. Teak was only shaken. Alan Green told him next time they would gallop together. Teak remembered the incident well, the look on Alan Green's face. A kind of pride in it.

Mounted and climbing slowly toward the ridge, Teak and Toma rode side-by-side as if suddenly comfortable together. Teak confined his talk to the mission, which was essentially interviewing a new warlord for the job of taking U.S. money and destabilizing the NSF. Most of Toma's clients asked where he was from and if he had family, and that was all. Just to get a rapport going. He could see it in their eyes, how it was good policy to make friends with the locals. But Teak was either too keyed into the job to think about it or didn't care. Toma surprised himself by volunteering the information.

"I'm from Zanzibar. Parents left Rwanda in sixty-nine. He was Somali, Hawiya, but she was a Tutsi, and pregnant."

"I'm from New York City," said Teak, knowing that Toma already knew.

"Home of the Velvet Underground." Toma smirked at him.

At the top of the ridge there was some cover and they stopped for lunch. The haze was lifting. They drank water. Teak took a pair of earbuds from his bag, plugged them into his phone, and played the Harlem Shakes and Ghengis Tron for Toma. Toma was unimpressed but they listened to two songs, each using a single earpiece, looking out over the troubled valley. They shared the avocado and bread Toma had brought along, and then Teak's energy bar.

A few miles after lunch they descended the opposite side of the ridge. When the path narrowed Toma told Teak they were nearly there. Between a pair of boulders they saw the mouth of a cave.

"No guard," said Toma in a warning tone. They tethered the horses and looked into the darkness of the cave. Satellites couldn't see through rock.

They ducked inside. The first chamber smelled of human sweat and old bush meat. In the middle was a circle of stones and a pot set on embers. There were some crates to the side, and mats by the far wall for sleeping. Teak tried to imagine how fierce and afraid he would have to be to retreat to such a place and he was now suddenly aware of a consistent *click-clacking* sound coming from what he guessed was another, deeper chamber. Teak and Toma looked at each other. Teak made a gesture to follow and stepped quietly around the smooth rock corner into the darkness. It was tar black. The air became cooler and Teak could tell that this chamber was larger than the first. He listened silently and heard breathing and more *click-clacking* through the darkness.

"Hello," he said, not wanting to surprise anyone. The *click-clacking* stopped. He could feel Toma at his shoulder.

Penlight from pocket. Teak switched it on. The chamber was a rough right triangle. A brown man in ragged canvas pants and a loose, torn shirt sat with his back to the hypotenuse. His head was shaved, pockmarked, scarred. On his right was a haphazard pile of perhaps fifty black nine-millimeter pistols. On his right were crates of broken down components for more guns. The man did not turn his face away from the light though Teak shone it directly in his eyes. He was blind, and held in his hands a half-assembled pistol.

25

Susan never liked parties. They made her nervous and she drank too much and men were always anxious to talk to her because she was beautiful, which sometimes made it worse. This party was different, of course, because she had been invited explicitly because she was so smart. But then, she was not feeling particularly smart.

A light dread had settled at her temples, a wired, tipsy feeling. There was no doubt she had been threatened that afternoon, with that CD. It made her look like a monster. It could have been put together any number of ways, she knew that. It made her think about the parts of herself that were low and murderous. Sometimes when she had been out with Hatashil she *had* wanted to kill all his enemies, to have her government drop great firebombs on them from the sky. She had always held this impulse in check, of course. But that didn't mean she was going to start enjoying parties.

The other Pulitzer winner, Tudo Denman, was standing by the door when she walked in, face slick with rain. Razi side-stepped Tudo and the attendant welcomers and headed straight for the bar. Susan tried to follow, but Tudo actually grabbed her by the arm and congratulated her on her achievement. Razi returned and handed her a glass of wine, then fled to the tall rain-streaked windows.

Two undergraduates in tuxedoes whom she didn't recognize stepped next to her and called for a picture. They shook hands in front of her. As the flash went off, Henry Rose arrived. He threw an arm around Tudo Denman and posed. He pulled the same move on Susan and she surprised him by leading him to a corner of the room. They were both tall enough to see over the crowd.

"I'm trying to do some more work on Hatashil, the so-called massacre."

"Don't worry, Susan, we're here for you on it. Even bad press lifts our profile."

Stupid old fuck, thought Susan. "I'm glad," she said. "But I wanted to know if you could help me get a meeting with the new national security director."

She could get a meeting herself but she wanted to speed it up and maybe Harrison would be looser if she came from Rose. She buttered him up. "You and Harrison are old friends, no? Wasn't there some story about the two of you racing your chauffeurs to St. Bernard's?"

"Yes, well," Rose laughed, pretending amusement but annoyed with Susan's knowing tone. "I'll see what I can do."

Susan felt better after she spoke with Rose. At least she had done something. She looked at her husband as he walked in.

He had the loose gait that Emily was already developing and the handsome open face that on Ford was still framed by baby fat. Often he appeared to her in the context of their children, and this pleasantly dammed her occasional desire to fuck other men. She knew that he thought about fucking other women, that on his third martini he discussed firmness and probable liquidity with like-minded colleagues—but also that he was a better man than them. And if he ever did paw a thigh in a town car en route to an afternoon hotel fuck, he would return to her exploded in grief. But neither of them would do it, or so she hoped, and this was why, she thought, they were married. Susan saw him bragging about her to someone by the door, even though it was a party in her honor. He loved her work, and she loved him for that.

On account of this work, the most they saw each other was in bed and during their periodic shopping sprees. After the initial infatuation, neither of them talked much about how they felt, as though through maintaining silence they could mold their marriage and themselves into a mellow, dignified, equilibrium. If we don't get into bullshit with each other, Susan had thought shortly before their small farmhouse marriage, then we will be people who don't deal in bullshit. As she passed the window, walking toward Harry, she glanced outside and saw Razi's familiar tweed shoulders, stooped and smoking under one of Corbusiers's concrete overhangs. She turned and stepped through the side door to huddle with him.

Razi was just then thinking how it would be if Susan were to walk outside. He had entertained these fantasies before. In hotels he had imagined her knocking on his door in the middle of the night, or better yet coming in through the window and into his bed. Camping out he had imagined her crawling into his thin sleeping bag. He had pictured them together in airplane bathrooms. Sometimes he tried to make himself stop. But not really. Thou shalt not covet meant nothing to him. He liked Harry but felt no harm no foul. Never before, however, had Susan actually appeared next to him right as he imagined her. They sheltered from the rain in silence.

"Can I . . ." said Susan.

He shook a Marlboro out of the pack for her, taking care to avoid the heavy rain drops. As he lit the cigarette she rested her long fingers on his hand around the Zippo, to protect the flame. Razi had always loved this gesture, almost no matter who did it. Something about the possibility of love and his love for cigarettes. But particularly when Susan did it. And she almost always did this when Razi lit her cigarettes, particularly when she was drunk. But he was sure she never thought about it.

"You know," she said, "you could have won this prize."

"I'm sure the medal will look better on you. Is it a medal, even, or what?"

"It's actually just a gift certificate to Barney's."

"I just tried to call Toma," said Razi, holding out his cell phone. "Line's been disconnected. All of them."

"Fuck."

Razi was always happy to have news for her, even bad news. He sometimes felt those were the only times when she really looked right at him. Though he was always looking at her. Susan was not even halfway through the cigarette when she flicked it away into the rain. "I have to use the ladies room."

* * *

She went to the basement where there was a bank of computers. She read the BBC article and stood there looking at it until Harry found her. He encircled her with his arms and read the screen over her shoulder.

"Shit," he said.

She decided not to tell him about the threat yet, and this decision made her tired. She insisted that they leave, even though Harry wanted to stay and said some bad news shouldn't ruin a good night.

"You're not even going to say good-bye to Razi?" Harry added.

"He'll understand."

Upstairs, Razi understood through several glasses of wine, and then understood himself to Daedalus. He regretted the choice but he didn't have it in him to walk the extra blocks to the Cellar. By last call he ran out of smokes and bummed a cigarette from an undergrad in a tuxedo. The undergrad had a friend, also in a tuxedo, and Razi was almost sure that he heard one say something to the other about "brown-skin brother" and "working the tobacco plantation."

He stared at them. "Excuse me?"

"Sorry there, quite rude not to introduce ourselves, isn't it, see you out all the time. I guess we're all sort of barflies. I'm Lucas." *Great,* thought Razi, *we're all sort of barflies.*

"And I'm Willy," said Willy. Razi shook hands with each of them and Lucas and Willy shook hands with each other. Razi declined Lucas and Willy's invitation to join them for "further revelry" and went home. He wished he was more sober and resolved not to drink with undergraduates.

* * *

Henry Rose tenderly hung up his suit, put his cuff links in their box, folded his pocket square on top of its brothers, and changed into striped pajamas. Then he called his old friend Mitchell Harrison, who was in New York to deliver a speech over lunch at the Council on Foreign Relations about calculated risk and rogue states.

"She asked for a meeting."

Harrison sighed into the phone from his suite at the Mark. "Fine." He watched the bathroom door, behind which a fifteen-hundred-dollar-an-hour twenty-seven-year-old call girl named Alexis was brushing her teeth. "I can do something with that. Thanks, Henry."

"Of course."

"Seriously, it's real work you're doing." Always good to lay it on him thick, thought Harrison. The girl was taking a long time in the bathroom.

"Oh, it's nothing," said Rose, allowing himself a smile at his importance. *Not just some crusty old academic.*

After Harrison got off the phone with Rose he called Alan Green and told him Susan Lowell wanted a meeting. Green told him that was fine, the package had been delivered, and signed off with something about another brick in the wall.

"I'd like to fuck her," said Harrison under his breath.

Through the door, Harrison could hear the hooker's cell phone ring. This disheartened him, shrinking away the half erection he had been nursing.

26

Teak had greeted the blind man in several languages, starting with Somali. The man said nothing. When Teak tried Arabic the man opened his mouth, gaping at the two of them, and Teak saw in the penlight beam that the man had no tongue. After a moment the man went back to assembling the pistols.

Teak and Toma walked back outside and decided to wait. They could still hear the *click-clack* of the gun assembly bouncing out of the cave. Sitting on the ground near the horses, Teak watched a pair of birds, too far off to identify, circling through the late afternoon light. Toma thought the men they were supposed to meet would be there by dark and there was at least an hour before then. Teak said he would take a walk along the ridge and have a look around.

"Nothing to see," said Toma, but Teak walked off anyway. A ways along the edge of the ridge, he could see the birds better. They were kites, clawing at each other high in the air. It was almost magnetic, repulse and attract. The birds looked awkward for an instant, as though they might fall from the sky.

Teak couldn't tell whether they were fighting or playing. *Fighting or playing.* The kites blended into the green and brown of the landscape as they dove below the horizon.

Thinking about Toma, Teak decided to stay away from the cave for an extra twenty minutes. *How he waits is a good test.* The sun was setting when Teak heard the shot. He returned carefully, finally crouching out of sight in the brush above the cave. Toma had been shot just above the knee and lay bleeding. The shooter stood over him. He had small eyes and a face that was weather-beaten and spongy with too much beer. This was not the man they had been expecting. He had with him a gang of young men in old fatigues. They were all armed and several of them were laughing at Toma grimacing on the ground.

Everything in Teak's training told him to take it all in and then *get out*. He looked at Toma, silent in the dirt, his thin face wet with perspiration and pain, his glasses grimed over. He would die. But first he would talk.

Teak pulled his SIG, jumped down from above the cave, and landed on his feet behind the small-eyed man, jamming his pistol to the man's head and wrapping his arm around his neck. The man smelled of old beer and a thick, salty grunge. Teak kicked the man's legs out from under him and forced him down to his knees. He accomplished this so quickly the gang was bewildered.

Teak told Toma to get on one of the horses and bring the other around to him. As Toma struggled to his feet Teak told the gang in their own language not to move and to drop their guns. One of the them said no but before he could train his gun on Toma the small-eyed man on his knees screamed at him, a high, blubbering sound. He told them to do what the white man said.

Toma painfully lifted himself onto the horse and the blood from his leg smeared the saddle. Teak yanked his hostage to his feet and, with the gun in his neck, prodded him into the saddle of the other horse and leapt up behind him. The men in fatigues shouted after them as they trotted off, the horses nervous along the narrow path.

"Are you with Hatashil?" Teak growled in the man's ear as they rode, now pressing the pistol between his ribs."

"Not anymore," said the man. "Please."

Two miles later Teak pushed the man from the horse and through the numbing pain in his leg Toma watched with satisfaction as the man bounced down the ridge.

"Thank you for not leaving," Toma said later that night. They were back in the room where Toma had woken Teak up that morning. Toma was drunk on whiskey. They could not get to a hospital that day and he lay tourniqueted on Teak's bed. Teak, sober, leaned out the window and looked at the dark shipping containers and the Indian Ocean beyond, thinking about the kites he had seen. *Fighting or playing*.

"Hey," said Toma from the bed. Teak turned from the window.

"The times, they are a-changing."

Every time Toma spoke a rock lyric, his eyebrows, which were long and thin like the rest of him, rose up and down. It suddenly occurred to Teak that Toma was mocking him, somehow, with the lyrics. He turned back to the window.

27

The CD had arrived at the *Crimson* that afternoon, addressed only to "Editor." Krazmeyer, in a frenzied, almost sexual excitement at the possibility of a national scoop, had called the five editors he trusted most. Now they stood on the balcony talking about what to do. Jane had insisted that everyone go out on the balcony so that the smokers could smoke as they talked. They all knew it was probably the biggest story they would see in college. Some of them were jealous it was going to be Jane's.

"It's not a crime for Lowell to say she believes in killing people," Jane said. "This is about discrediting her."

"Her Pulitzer could get pulled back," said Krazmeyer. "It's simple, the freedom fighter is a warlord, and Lowell got it wrong. She made us all believe, she even got the divestment movement started. She's been all over the press, she's practically the white face of Africa!"

"We don't know where the CD came from," interjected one of the other editors.

"We know we have it, and she'll have to respond to us," said Krazmeyer. "And the national press will definitely pick it up." He turned to Jane, "You just have to get the story right."

"I'll get it right."

We are all just so fucking important, thought Jane.

That evening Jane and David sat on Jane's bed. The window looking out on Mount Auburn Street was shut against the fall chill and they leaned into each other and watched the CD with Susan Lowell's voice.

"I don't think she would say that," said David.

"She's saying it right there," Jane tapped her laptop.

"I wish you weren't the one to write this story," said David.

"Well, I am. So you'll have to give me a statement. You're as close to her as any of her students."

"No!"

"Nothing is black and white," Jane tried to reason. "She might have made things up in her book. If she doesn't care about casualties, you don't think she might fudge things?"

David remembered a neighbor from home who constantly fingered the hole where his ear had been. He was tall and had smiled gap-toothed at David all through his childhood, teased him about becoming a doctor. This man wore all his clothes two sizes too big, flowing beneath his beanpole neck. David recalled tugging on his baggy shirts from behind and then running off.

David's father had explained what happened, though not why. The NSF men had held him down, hands on skull, skull on tire, him screaming, pleading, and sliced his left ear off, but it didn't come off cleanly so fingers pinched the top of it, fingers connected to a hand connected to a man, and the man had ripped the ear off. Another man had said *slave ear!*

"So stay out of trouble," was how David's father ended the story.

"No statement," said David.

Jane was tired. She'd try again later. She closed the laptop and lay down with her head in David's lap.

Jane and David lay in her bed together, entwined, talking about the summer internships. Jane had access to a great number of them, at Sotheby's if she wanted, more likely at *Vanity Fair* again, although she was thinking of doing more charity work, or maybe some kind of nonprofit thing. For her, it was as natural and simple as attending college in the first place. Not so for David. He had no connections, and she hadn't offered hers. He thought if he got into the club someone in it could get him an internship.

And I need one, he thought. Because if he didn't get one of those jobs after college—and you needed an internship to get one, everyone agreed—then what would he do? Educated but so what? Speaking three languages but so what? Went to Harvard but so what? He needed to get what the actual Harvard kids got. Not just be there, abroad, away from home, alien and not rewarded for it.

Jane had fallen asleep. He was glad she hadn't brought up the Susan Lowell story again. He had bigger problems. He felt the fine bones of Jane's ankles slide off his calves as he got out of bed. She snored softly now, as he leaned over the desk in the light of her computer screen, double-checking his summer internship applications.

28

The waves seemed to break almost silently. Days passed and Teak grew more and more restless watching the purple and gold clouds floating up to his *banda* from Yemen. In the evenings he drank with Francisco, who revealed nothing of his history. Teak was confused by Francisco's relationship with Lunt but would have been unsurprised by Francisco's trajectory from Madrid by way of a coffee plantation called Haddada Ranch in Kenya's Happy Valley. Francisco perceived Teak to be extremely guarded and recently unlucky.

That morning Teak sailed a Sunfish out of the inlet and around the leeward side of the island, past the main building where they ate. He watched a skate swim beneath him through the clear water and considered how the white sandy bottom resembled the sand dunes of the Sahara, which he had seen only through the scratched window of an airplane. He sailed perhaps three miles around the island and beached the Sunfish. When he had pulled it above the tide line he set off into the vegetation without intention. He was gratified when he saw a family of gray and blue monkeys of a species unfamiliar to him grooming each other on a fallen tree.

Teak had wanted to be a biologist. The joys of Central Park had been exquisite and varied for him when, as a boy, he would crawl on all fours through the grass of the Great Lawn, fascinated by the insect life. In school he had appreciated the study of cells but his passion was reserved for zoology. He did not anthropomorphize the animals he admired but he ascribed to them a kind of cosmic intelligence, which he believed was more than Darwinian. Having seen, on safari, three young lions kill and fight over a lamed eland, he had dreamed of it regularly. The others in his truck that day had been fascinated, too, but Teak believed that he might have spent years following those lions and studying their lives, though such study had already been done by better qualified men. He felt that the cruelty of men was grotesque, whereas the cruelty of animals was somehow a relief and he wanted to study it. But that wasn't important enough work he had decided.

The monkeys scattered as Teak heard an airplane coming in close above him, obviously landing on the island. The famous couple was not to leave for several days so it was either supplies from the mainland or new guests. Under the roar Teak had a premonition that Francisco might spy on him in his *banda*, maybe bug the place if he hadn't already. When the plane noise died Teak became aware of another sound, a rustling human noise.

He followed the sound and through a curtain of hanging vines saw the three-walled schoolhouse and the cleared field.

He had not realized that he had already walked so far inland. The noise was still faint but he followed it to the schoolhouse, where he saw Maria lying naked from the waist down, her legs spread in the shade of the building. One of Francisco's cooks had one hand on her and his other hand on his cock. Maria's face was twisted and flushed. She might have been grabbing for the cook's cock, too, Teak couldn't quite see. He ran to the scene, shouted at the cook to get away from her.

Maria began to cry and the cook fled into the green pulling up his pants. Teak turned to Maria and knelt to ask if she was hurt but Maria only cried, sometimes softly and sometimes releasing great guttural sobs. As Teak coaxed her back into her jeans, she opened her huge reddened eyes and roared at him. He stepped back for a moment, and Maria's ferocity faded as quickly as it had burst out. She hung her head. Teak took her elbow and walked her to the road and then toward the main house.

Maria continued to cry as they walked. When they heard the approach of a truck behind them, Teak took her to the side of the road and as the open truck came into view they saw the driver who had chauffeured Teak. In the back seat was Francisco and, next to him, Lunt. Maria, as she always did when she saw him, waved to her father.

29

Lucas and Willy stood in the opportune twilight outside the Spee Club's famous pajama party. They wore cummerbunds, bowties, cuff links, tuxedo jackets, and boxer shorts, but no pants. One of the crowd of girls waiting for entrance turned to them.

"The tuxedo guys," she said. She wore silver panties and a silver bra, a sheer shawl, high heels, and pink rabbit ears. They bowed simultaneously.

The bass pumped from inside the club. They followed the girls out of the cold fall air and into the sticky, humid basement. Sepia photographs hung from the wood-paneled walls. In the corner a giant stuffed bear roared toward the ceiling, threatening the chandelier. Everywhere were women in their underwear, men in boxer shorts and tank tops.

"Look Lucas," said Willy, "I think we need to set that bear on fire."

"That may not help me get laid," cautioned Lucas.

Lucas found the rabbit-eared freshman and led her toward the back door.

"So, what classes are you taking?" he asked.

"I'm taking Susan Lowell's Africa core class, but I'm starting to think she's full of shit. You know she was a accused of plagiarism or something—"

A southpaw pitcher from Florida bumped into her and she spilled her beer on the carpet.

"It's fine," he said, "they'll get it tomorrow. Come with me, I'll show you something wild."

Lucas didn't want to lose the freshman to the southpaw. And the night's weed—*fuck knows where Willy got this batch*—seemed to be laced with something. Everything was pulsing. He plowed on.

"Race and ethnicity are crucial," he said to the girl, grabbing a beer from the bar as they walked out into the garden. Willy was already there, standing in a ring of club members passing around a bowl. Lucas and Willy greeted each other with a handshake, and the freshman girl typed a text message into her phone.

"What's the trick you brought me out here to see?" the freshman girl asked, lighting a cigarette.

The southpaw was outside, too, taking an apple from a plastic bag on the garden table. He walked to the far side of the garden and faced the wall of the building.

"He's gonna vaporize that shit," someone said.

The pitcher wound up but Willy shouted, "Wait! Trick like this needs an introduction. I want you all to look up at the moon." A crowd, sensing entertainment, was now gathering around them. Willy had given speeches like this before.

"So, we have been reading the classics . . . the greatest

minds of my generation destroyed by madness and greed . . . wielding spiked clubs to beat us into television personalities . . . They try to drive us into church . . . drive us from drink . . . drive us from everything that is decent and holy in our fat purple mountains majesty and *semper* fucking *fi*. And the International House of Pancakes, you see, they can't take this away from me . . . the red hills of Georgia and my New York City queer poets and my Hebrews arriving by great fucking zeppelin . . . miniature planes falling around us and exploding on the waters . . . they send us after ghosts in head towels . . . and where are my Negro brothers? Let us turn the Maxim guns away from them for a change, it has been long coming but it is not too late . . . only a blip on our upward population growth when the ripeness is all, then is aller. And Allah says? Nothing you fool, Dre is dead, I locked him in my basement."

Much laughter. Who knew what the fuck Willy was saying, but he was making a fool of himself, and that was funny. Then the southpaw, with a tipsy but ferocious athleticism, hurled the apple into the wall. The apple exploded into mist and the crowd in the garden cheered.

Lucas asked the freshman girl if she wanted to take a walk.

They went upstairs to the kitchen. Lucas had guessed it would be empty, and he was right. The kitchen gleamed, clean and big and silver, professional-grade appliances and knives and bowls. Lucas turned in front of the sink and kissed the girl. She kissed him back.

"You know, he's my best friend," he said into her hair, "but he is fucking crazy."

"I don't know," said the girl, "I sort of thought he was making sense."

They waltzed and made out into the pantry. They smelled the comforting dryness of powdered stock and cardboard over cornflakes and cans and stacked boxes of pasta. The room reminded them both of their childhoods and they made out more fervently.

"Yeah," she said catching her breath, "like that famine stuff. I'm taking a class on that, too."

"What do you think?" asked Lucas.

"The same stuff over and over again," said the girl.

"You want to take a walk?" said Lucas.

30

The day's first birdsong competed with the delivery trucks. David had been struggling with his paper on John Stuart Mill all night and was falling asleep at his desk when he heard the *sshh* of an envelope sliding under his door. He jumped up and hurried across the room to pick it up. Wax seal, his name handwritten. He had made the cut. In that second he wanted to open the door to see who had delivered the note, to find some insight into the secret machinations that went into this process, this institution. He wanted to do that very badly but he held himself back. He did not want to risk some kind of faux pas, some mark against him, being too curious. *Just a guy dropping off a note, anyway*. He sat down at his desk and ever so carefully opened the envelope. *Bring a change of clothes,* it read, *to the appointed place, at the appointed time.*

The event began in front of Kirkland House the next Sunday morning. David arrived fifteen minutes before the specified time, planning to take a walk by the river and loop back around, so as not to be seen as too early. But there were already half a dozen young men in coats and ties milling about and exhaling small puffs of cold air at one another. More arriving.

Robert showed up, wearing dark glasses. David rushed up to him and explained that he hadn't meant to lose him at the last event, he was just in the middle of a drink you know? Pleased that David had been thinking about this, Robert said only that he was *fockin'* hungover.

They noticed Spencer staring at them. Then the group of young men divided, surprised, as a bus with tinted windows rolled up behind them. Robert waved and smiled and said "Hello, you great wanker," though no one heard him but David.

Everyone got on the bus and the ride was quiet. Many of the boys were tired, and many were hungover. The city gave way to suburbs and then to the late fall trees. The remaining leaves were varicolored and distinct. Some of the boys slept.

David leaned his head on the window and felt the chill. People said Africans didn't like the cold. He even knew Africans who always made a big joke about how cold it was here in America, how it wasn't for them. But that was all nonsense, he thought. He liked the cold. He liked the houses that looked so warm and inviting, dotted among the woods and hills as they dove through western Massachusetts. He liked that there was no one walking along the road with nowhere to go, nothing to do. It was too cold for that here, you couldn't just shuffle around all day. Maybe that was why the Northern Hemisphere was the way it was. Professor Lowell had called this theory "that old racist chestnut" on the first day of class.

Finally, the bus slowed and turned off the road to a gate. One of the club members riding with them—he had sat by himself in the front, sleeping the whole way—got out of the bus and pressed a button on a post by the gate, which then swung open. Down the long gravel driveway, David looked out at the thick thorny undergrowth. Nothing was manicured, New England brush right up to the edge of the driveway.

They parked in a gravel lot beside a barn with three closed bay doors. Shaking the stiffness from their legs, Robert and David followed the rest of the boys following the sleepy club member. They walked down a flagstone path to a wooden fence overgrown with ivy. Through the gate, they came to the house, which rose suddenly three stories above them and sprawled out beyond their vision. Here, the grounds were manicured. In front of the porch was a stone patio with iron furniture that looked out on a great, perfectly kept lawn that ran slightly downhill to a pond and a weeping willow. Beyond the pond the morning mist was just now burning off on the dark pine hills. In the middle of the lawn, David saw a foursome playing croquet.

"Is that cro-fockin'-quet?" Robert muttered incredulously.

A middle-aged black man approached them with a silver tray of Bloody Marys.

"Cheers," said Robert as he picked up one of the tall glasses and drank off the top.

David declined and considered asking for an orange juice at the bar. Everyone else seemed to be drinking alcohol.

It was the crowd from the previous event, but halved. And there were different older men, one of whom, a stoop-shouldered white-haired man in a hunting jacket, seemed to be the owner of the property. His old blue eyes lit up as he shook hands with each of the young men, and he grilled them about what they were studying and where they were from and "how the Cliffies were behaving this year."

The crowd drifted inside and when Robert went to the bar for the third time, David split off. He scanned the room for Alan Green or Jackson Oliver and didn't see either. But then he was saved. Someone they had introduced him to re-introduced himself and took David around. Many people asked him about his home, and no matter what he said they seemed interested. David felt like he was making a good impression.

Waiters laid out an elaborate brunch of various meats, vegetables, eggs, fruit, and a number of sauces. Others filled coffee cups and passed cream. David noticed, as he began eating baby asparagus spears between some of his new acquaintances, that Robert was sitting by himself at the end of another table. He didn't look like he minded, though, eating and drinking with relish. David wished Robert would sit next to some people and talk.

At the end of the meal the club member from the front of the bus *tink*ed his glass with his fork and announced a touch football game for those who wished to join in. David decided immediately that he would play. He glanced at Robert and was surprised to see him in conversation with the white-haired owner of the property. They were not listening to the football announcement.

The boys all changed clothes in the gun room and tramped down to the lawns. David did not enjoy football. Though physically he was an ideal wideout, he was nervous and didn't know the rules well. But he knew the game wasn't really about the game. It was about getting into the club. It was about a code, a specific dance.

Robert joined the game late and whacked the shit out of everybody. "Fockin' Americans," he shouted, "this is supposed to be your game."

As the boys lined up for the bus back to Cambridge, a black Mercedes pulled up the long gravel driveway. David was at the end of the line and he saw Alan Green step out from behind the wheel. David wished Green had been there earlier, so they could've spoken during the actual event. And then Green waved to him. David waved back, pleased that his fellow punches noted the interaction. David was still waving when he realized that, in fact, Green was waving for him to come over to the car. David hurried over, feeling like an idiot.

"Want a ride back to school?" asked Green.

Alan Green had seen some evil in his life. He had seen murder, the quick departure of a man's soul from his body (sweating, lashed to a splintered chair and beaten) before the ruined eyes of the man's sister. He had never taken pleasure in being party to such departures, or the suffering that often preceded them, but he believed in their necessity. There was, he told himself, a difference between himself and the Belarusian in Athens, for example, who famously kept a jar of thumbs in formaldehyde next to a jar of pickled eggs that he ate as he wrote reports. Green considered himself a professional and what misgivings he did have about his work were not fundamental but rather, as he put it, "floating frothy on the top of the cold American milk of my convictions." He was deeply cynical and afraid to retire and become, as he said with a sneer to his wife, someone who *spends all day looking at things*.

Green drove fast through the Massachusetts countryside, talking the whole time: Harvard, Africa, Washington, New York, Hollywood. David felt like he was getting a view of the world he hadn't considered. The point was: reasonable men can control an unreasonable world. Not something David had ever thought about, but listening to Green it began to make a kind of sense.

"You can drive a stick I bet," Green said to David. "No one drives stick anymore. It's too bad. You understand the machine better, and hell, it's more fun."

David could drive manual because there were so few automatics where he was from. Everyone who drove drove manual, along bad roads that ended abruptly, like chopped off fingers. Then you switched gears. He chose not to point this out to Green. Maybe driving manual was also more fun.

"Have you ever driven a Mercedes?" asked Green. He was already pulling over under an emptying elm, smallest branches like latticework against the sky. "Want to?"

No. "Yes, thanks." As David worked uneasily up into third gear, Green looked out the window. Then he turned and David could feel the older man's eyes on him and was glad he had to look at the road instead of Green.

"You're one of Susan Lowell's advisees, aren't you?" he questioned.

"Yes," said David, wondering how Green knew this. "She's a very good advisor."

"Do you think she did it," Green asked.

"What?"

"Loyalty only goes so far, David."

"I'm sorry, I just don't know what you're asking about."

"Apparently, Hatashil insisted that she kill a prisoner if she was to stay and have access to him."

David wanted to say this was crazy, but he didn't. He thought of Professor Lowell in her office, marking up one of his essays.

"I've never heard that," said David. "Hatashil never did things like that."

"Real good book, though," remarked Green, "for a while."

David nodded, keeping his eyes on the road.

David had been looking forward to seeing Jane that afternoon. She would be a relief from the stress of the punch event. But after the strange ride with Green he felt spacey, airheaded. He went to her room and found her organizing her clothes.

"I don't want to be wearing safari gear," she said after she kissed him on the cheek.

"I must have forgotten," David said. He hadn't forgotten but neither had he been thinking about it. He had hoped that ignoring her trip would suggest to Jane that she was no more important than his punch event, or applications for summer internships, or classes. He had wanted to make her jealous of him with his busy life but now knew he could not and felt crippled by this.

"I heard something really crazy about Professor Lowell today," David began, and related what Alan Green had told him.

"Hold on," said Jane, when he had finished. She opened her laptop. "Say all that again."

"You can't—"

"David, please. Your name won't be anywhere."

David remembered the look on Professor Lowell's face last week in her office, when she had told him how much she hated the NSF. He hesitated.

"It's just background, David," said Jane, crossing her legs under her on the bed and getting ready to type. "I'm not going to do anything wrong."

31

Teak sailed slowly over the glassy water. The sun had just set and the wind was dying. Reclining port-side, Lunt lit a cigarette and smoked. Teak was displeased to see Lunt flick his butt into the clear water when he finished.

"I want you to know that we had no idea that was coming down." Lunt was earnest, declarative.

"Ready about," said Teak. Lunt's lie somehow inspired him to change direction. Though he tried not to, he thought of the Fanta kid.

Lunt lit another cigarette. The wind picked up slightly and Teak eased off onto a broad reach, skimming over the ripples away from land. Nothing lay before them but the Indian Ocean. Teak related his meeting with Hatashil.

"So, who do you think they were?" said Lunt, thinking it was good this kid hadn't gotten killed. *Fucking Alan Green*. On balance, Lunt figured, Teak's death would be worse for his career, though his survival presented certain headaches. *And shit, I didn't want the kid to die*.

“The only name I got was Blackford. He was American. The others not, but gear like ours.”

“We’re the fucking Americans,” Lunt said.

Teak was surprised at the sudden anger in Lunt’s voice as he went off on how the situation was all fucked up, he didn’t like it, and Teak was going home. He’d have a month for a graceful exit from Nairobi and to prep the control agents for hand over. This Hatashil assignment was totally over. Too fucked up. Lunt softened his tone at the end of the speech.

“And whatever happened out there, Teak, it’s not on you. It’s not on us. It’s over now.”

Teak, thinking of the Fanta kid, felt better to hear Lunt say this. Because he knew that he would obey orders. He always did. And yet he felt, at the same time, some flicker in his chest, shame at his relief.

“Turn this thing around,” said Lunt, flicking his second cigarette into the sea. “Let’s get back on the fucking land.”

32

The day was bright and blustery and the leaves were piled in the gutters like shreds of the reams of essays that the students turned out. Students other than Lucas and Willy. They walked to Daedalus for steaming eggs, heaped with salmon. Lucas, for his part, was extremely happy to be alive. His hangover was positive, Willy's negative. *This is how life is,* he thought, congratulating himself on his perspicacity. *Life is beautiful.* And he was looking forward to Europe over the vacation, and après-ski. The sex last night had been too drunken for him to remember the awkwardness of it. *Those freshmen from Darien,* he thought. Glad she was from there, he hadn't tried to being gentle or anything like that, they just banged. Another discovery of—

"Christ, a cigarette, before the clean air kills me," shouted Willy, interrupting Lucas's thoughts.

"Have you not seen those new ads?" asked Lucas, handing over a silver cigarette case. "With the pumping heart and disintegrating lung and the fat cancer man?"

"Hahahahah," laughed Willy. He was jealous that Lucas had fucked that freshman from the pajama party. He laughed like a madman.

"Hahahahah," Lucas started laughing, imitating him. Willy could be really fucking crazy sometimes.

"*Hahahaha,*" howled Willy.

They stood there, imitating laughter at each other. Then the imitation turned into real laughter, and they were swept up, doubled over, they couldn't stop laughing. Tears squeezed out of Willy's eyes, and as he laughed he was hacking, too, because he was smoking, and finally he was laughing so hard he had to throw away the cigarette.

33

Razi stood in front of a bulletin board in Harvard Yard. He often lingered before the boards, perusing the student-group flyers. An old source on the Al-Emudi story had left him a voice mail earlier that evening. Just a name and instructions to call back. Razi looked up the name and discovered that the man in question was an accessory to Al-Emudi's plot to rob the DMI Trust and various Islamic banks, and had just been murdered in Somalia, which didn't make any sense. Why would he be in the Horn and not in the south of France? It was too hard to think about it. Instead of calling the source back Razi had gone out for a drink. A woman at the bar had told him she was a nurse. Razi had thought about Susan Lowell. The woman had kept talking about her patients. Razi had decided she was not a good nurse and left the bar. And now he swayed in front of the bulletin board, considering whether or not he should go back and see what could happen with the nurse.

"Fuck it," he said, as he looked at the posters. His attention rested on one for the Boston Africa Action Group conference. Brunch and brainstorming, workshops.

"Fuck her."

The next morning Razi woke up still buzzed and walked to the Boston Africa Action Group conference, which was being held in Sever Hall in Harvard Yard. The conversation with the nurse was forgotten.

Inside, almost everyone was a teenager. Razi ignored the sign-up sheet, passed the blonde girl in the green T-shirt who was encouraging her peers to network, and walked straight to the food. The muffins were plastic and he ate two. The orange juice was cool and sweet and he drank it down fast.

In the auditorium he sat near the stage, eavesdropping on the networkers, and decided if he heard anymore about sleep deprivation while he was on this campus he would, well, he would go and have another fucking drink. The crowd was all white but for him, an Afro guy, and the law student from the University of Khartoum who would speak later in a thick accent. Razi watched the local queen of the thin humanitarian women—joint law/policy degree, breasts, been in the field, unidentifiable Anglo accent—dazzle the undergrads. Divestment. Frustration. Hope. But no talk of the recent news, no talk about Hatashil's massacre.

Razi's instincts as a reporter overcame his incoming hangover. He raised his hand. The humanitarian queen pointed at him. "Yes, there's a question?"

"Thank you," said Razi. "I wanted to know if we, as the Boston Africa Action Group, have any reaction to the recent news concerning Hatashil and the U.S.'s new support for Al-Kateb?"

After relating their chief analyst's résumé she told him that it was such a recent development that the committee hadn't reached a conclusion yet, but that it would influence support strategies. And that it was a great question, especially to address in the workshops.

Well, thought Razi, *what the fuck was I expecting.*

The student leader—nondescript, dumpy—gave the queen a long hug when she finished. She was in awe of the queen, hoped to have a similar career. She thought the queen was cool; the student leader had actually been to Africa, gone because she believed. To Razi, it looked as though the student leader actually wanted to ingest the queen, amoeba-like.

After the hug, the student leader said, "There will be a break for thirty minutes, we're a little ahead of schedule. And really, cross the room to get to know each other, because some of you have come from a ways off, and that's so great, and so you should just go up and introduce yourself to that guy from Northeastern," she pointed randomly at a guy in a windbreaker, "because he's just a person like you, and that's what we're doing here, because the people in Africa, whether they're here or not, they could just be across the room, and that's what we're trying to do here."

That afternoon Razi took a walk along the river before he went to the bar. He thought about what he could ever really know—nothing—and whether he should have ever become a journalist. At the bar, he decided there were only three solid sources of information. The bartender—rockabilly, slicked-back hair, black glasses—who was in conversation about the ruthless efficiency and historical excellence of patriots; the television, which was tuned to college football; and Razi's own face, reflected in the mirror. *Tired, old, hungover.*

He recalled being in the Senate office building during his own college days in D.C. and asking an aide one of those stupid young questions that turns out to be profound: "Where does the information come from, for policy making?" The aid told him to think of it as a finite number of sources for any given policy maker. Intelligence organizations, think tanks, public pressure. But, of course, said the aide, the information tends to fit whatever the policy is. So, in a sense, it's better to have fewer sources of information to deal with. *Today,* thought Razi, *I will focus my attention on the television and have exploratory conferences with the bartender, representing my top-shelf constituents.*

When Razi became a real drinker, even though he was just a junior at Georgetown, he had worried that the booze would make his hair fall out. His scalp had itched. He used to watch for the wisps in the sink. On his third drink, in the condensation of memory on the outside of his Maker's rocks, he recalled how one day he just stopped worrying about his hair falling out. He laughed out loud at the memory.

"How you doin'?" asked the bartender.

"I've got limited information," said Razi.

Bless me with the capacity for kindness, he thought, and asked for another drink.

34

Even though Susan Lowell had asked for the meeting, Director Harrison had insisted on meeting in her office, to "see the famous author's desk." She found this aggressive and creepy. She had wanted to meet in the Kennedy School, in one of the small conference rooms. But Harrison also said he wanted to say hello to his best old friend Henry Rose down the hall afterward. So that was another reason. It was as if a shitty date had insisted on picking up the tab and then followed her home. Except, of course, she had asked for the meeting.

Harrison sat with his legs crossed tightly and smiled at her without showing his teeth. They spoke for a while about Susan's brothers, who had attended the same prep school as Harrison's children and were their contemporaries. None of Harrison's children had followed their father into the Foreign Service and this saddened him. He had thought about it again at the club the night before, while having a scotch by the fire.

He wished he and Susan Lowell could have their talk—who was he kidding, it was an interview—at the club. He had often wished he could bring women there. His turf. But it was against the rules. Women weren't allowed in the club until they'd been married to a member for twenty-five years, and even then it was rare. He'd never brought his wife.

Susan did not have much history with Harrison. She had met him only once at a think tank reception. He hadn't been important to her work until now. She knew that she should not be plowing ahead without cultivating him, learning him. This was her peculiar skill, the reporter's sense of pacing: when she could ask a question, when she couldn't. But she needed to know things. And in the end it wasn't about friendship at all.

When he congratulated her on the Pulitzer, as she had known he would she thanked him and asked him directly if he had heard anything about Hatashil recently.

As he told her he knew they didn't always agree politically, but that he knew they agreed about one thing, a cloying earnestness came into his voice. She had heard it before from senators, guerrilla revolutionaries, thieves in Nairobi, priests, rabbis, *roshi*s in Tokyo, astrologers, architects, terrorists, movie producers at the Chateau Marmont, police and firefighters, her family, successful novelists, beggars, cab drivers, once an astronaut.

Susan laughed. "What's that?"

"We both love this country."

"Of course," she said. "And we would do anything to protect it. But nothing that subverts what we're trying to protect."

"You have a flexible mind."

She nearly interrupted him but he went on about how it was about more than the lives of Americans and that these people actually wanted to destroy freedom. They wanted to extinguish every point of light around the world. They wanted silence and fear. They wanted women subjugated. It was about protecting the possibility of a life like hers. Otherwise there could be no one like her.

"No you." He was leaning forward in his chair.

Susan set her teeth and paused to keep the distaste off her face. She asked what his speech in the Kennedy School the previous week had to do with Hatashil, exactly.

"We have reason to believe that Hatashil has links to al-Qaeda." Harrison spat the words out.

"Really? I thought he was fighting a civil war."

"He's not what he claims to be."

"Well, what is he then? Off the record."

"This is all off the record," Harrison said sharply. "I know all you people want him to be a freedom fighter but he's not. And we know that he never was what he claimed to be. Even in the beginning. Put another way, the NSF and Al-Kateb are not good, but given what we know, they are better than Hatashil."

"He's not killing civilians." She felt stupid as she said it. But she was furious and had to know what Harrison knew. "I grant you," she said, recovering, "he is a bandit of sorts."

"Susan," said Harrison, "*I* am not a bandit." His eyes hardened and he leaned even closer to her, concentrating his energy. "And let me tell you this, *off the record*. I like you, Susan. I think you are a smart, decent woman. So if you have anybody left with him, if there are any *blonde hairs* left over there, friends, colleagues, anything cooking, anything that has ever touched this *terrorist* . . . " Harrison stopped and leaned back, looking at her. Then he stood up. "Congratulations on the Pulitzer, professor," he said, and turned and walked out.

* * *

Susan was still at her desk staring out the window five minutes later when there was knock at her door.

"Come in," she said.

Harrison muttered that he had left his briefcase. It lay against the chair where he had been sitting. He bent for it and then was out the door again. Susan wanted to laugh but no laugh came and she went back to staring out the window.

35

Teak was tuned in to death before he saw it up close, and then seeing it tuned him in tighter. He didn't understand death. No one does, maybe, until they are dead themselves. But some people are on the frequency and Teak knew early that he wanted to see it up close, wipe the blood from his forehead.

Conquer it, beat it. That was what he always tried to do, wanted to do. *What a nightmare,* part of him thought, *to be a good soldier,* to like it when everything sped up and there was no room for thought. To be interested in death. Good at it. But the greater nightmare: to be bad at it. To get panicky and hysterical. *To have died the first time*.

Even leaving Teak's parents out of it—because everyone has parents, cancers and shaking hands, the plasticine death rituals of modern health care—his bones were picking up the death vibrations. He always saw the tendons under the skin. Appreciated the infinite possibilities, the flora and fauna's bottomless capacity to swallow man up, consume him. He thought that he would have to be close to death for a long time to understand it and he thought that was dangerous, could make him crazy. Seeing a few bodies didn't do it, that was like seeing movies, except you were there. That's how it was for Teak, all the time.

The morning Toma got out of the hospital they were driving out of Nairobi when a raggedy kid jumped in front of the Land Cruiser. All snot and tears and high. The bottle of glue in his shirt under his chin shifted a little bit every time his heart beat. So he was breathing the glue all the time, with every breath. And he screamed at Toma to "give me some fucking money from the *mzungu* because you can see I have nothing and he has everything and why are you driving this *mzungu* and give me. GIVE TO ME." He held his hand out, palm up, shook his other hand at them, and Teak drove the car forward slowly. But the kid would not get out of the way and he wailed at them.

Teak's frequency. He saw the kid on the same spectrum as he had seen the child with the Fanta shard blown away at Hatashil's village. And he had words to say to the glue-head about *mzungus* and economics and all of that but none of it seemed as important as the immediacy of the glue breaking down the kid's medulla, the bullet ripping open the chest of the Fanta kid. And he had words about how every time he saw someone light a cigarette he was a little bit closer to facedown, and every time he saw someone driving a car, crashed lungs. And what could he say about that? Nothing. So he drove around the glue-head and looked straight at him. Just a beggar he saw while he was working.

"You know what the government in Nairobi says about hitting someone in the street?" Toma asked as they got clear of the glue-head.

Teak did know. Everyone knew. In the official tourist embassy warning literature it said: "Don't stop if you hit someone in the street because their friends will hijack you. Drive on. You will not be prosecuted."

Except that you will, Teak suddenly thought as Toma finished. *We all will*. And the thought frightened him, and he pushed it away.

Toma glanced over at Teak as they left the beggar kid behind, and smiled to himself. Teak was staring, space-eyed, straight ahead through the windshield. That story, Toma thought, it always gets them.

36

Susan was on her roof again, drinking a glass of wine. She had been furious since her meeting with Harrison. Her phone rang, a reporter named Jane Baker from the *Crimson,* asking for a statement about Hatashil's massacre and new rumors that she herself had executed a prisoner in exchange for access. It was surreal.

"I did what?" she demanded.

Jane Baker was determined not to be intimidated and explained that a group of Professor Lowell's own students had asked the *Crimson* to investigate the rumor because, even though they did not want their grades in her classes to suffer, they nonetheless felt they had a responsibility and—

"I'll give you a comment when you all fucking grow up," Susan interrupted, and hung up.

After that, she turned off her phone and her BlackBerry so she could just think about Hatashil, put the pieces together. Harrison was clearly lying . . . Toma was incommunicado . . . the BBC report . . . that weird release from State. And now this rumor about her executing a prisoner. *Maybe it's better not to think.*

When she finished her wine, she turned her phone back on, regretting her outburst at the reporter. She couldn't believe she had done that. She ought to call the *Crimson* and ask to speak to her. But now she saw that she had one unheard message. It was from Chairman Henry Rose, about what he called "the situation." It would all blow over, he was sure; he had no questions at all about her integrity, but with the recent media attention, and the continuing scrutiny of Harvard's African and African American studies departments, there was really no way to avoid it. They couldn't have the department supporting Hatashil's massacre. It was all too sensitive. *Practically Holocaust politics.*

The committee would be as discreet as it could be, but they would need all of her notes. If they were going to bat for her, to defend the book, they had to have their bases covered.

PART III

Nairobi, Kenya, 200X

Teak almost never drinks, but he buys a liter of gin and now, in the tar of 4 a.m., he sits cross-legged on the floor of his small bedroom, back to the bed, looking at the five empty Fanta cans he has arranged in front of him. The bottle of gin is almost empty. He pours the last of it into the plastic cup with some more Fanta and rises, unsteadily, to look out the window into the hot, smoggy night. He realizes that his cigarette is burning the top of his thumb. He holds on indifferently, as his skin burns and the cigarette dies, before he flicks it out into the street. He opens the drawer of his desk by the window and takes out his pistol.

"This," he says, nodding, "is bad judgment."

He turns and slumps back down to the floor. "So goddamn . . ." he gesticulates with the gun, talking to himself, gently bouncing his back against the side of the bed. "A couple of bodies and you can't hold it together." He raises his eyebrows and looks at the gun in his hand as though surprised to find it there. "Need to unload the gun."

He releases the clip from the pistol and thumbs out a bullet.

"One." He stands the bullet on top of one of the Fanta cans. "I was given much." He pushes another bullet from the clip and stands it on the next can. "Two. I am good at my job. Three," he hesitates with the third bullet, but then places it. "I am not good at my job tonight."

He laughs and then frowns.

"Four. Not just a couple of bodies, a whole village. Nuance." He sways as he goes on, talking fast. "Right. And here you are, drunk, and can't even get to five, talking to yourself, asshole." He is slurring his words. He takes a deep breath and lights another cigarette. "Tomorrow, work. And tonight," he puts the barrel of the gun to his thumb, "burned thumb." He forces himself to his feet again. He checks the lock on his door, puts the pistol back in the drawer, and though it takes him a long time, he sets the alarm clock. Then he passes out, face up, on the bed he made.

37

After that first night back from Funzi, when Teak got drunk and talked to himself, he rose early in the morning. He was embarrassed by his binge, his insecure talking out loud, and resolved to be strong and healthy for the rest of his time in Nairobi. *Defenses up*.

Waking before dawn he went for a run. He hadn't run like this since college, when he had abandoned the treadmills and their war televisions for the path along the river. Friends called him a tough motherfucker for running in the cold, and seeing this new run some might have called him crazy, or reckless, a slow-moving target in the predawn dark of Nairobi. But he was running for himself, and the run eased his hangover. By the time he finished the pink sun had broken greasy and golden over the Nairobi skyline, and greasier lower down over the tin-sea slums of Kibera, Mathare, Korogocho. He would repeat the run in the coming mornings, as a kind of talisman against hard days. Because he had to tell his agents he was leaving. Teak hated it. None of them were surprised. Spies had left before, told them the same things. Nothing changed. Every day, urchins and hawkers still tried to bag Teak until he surprised them with his Swahili. The difference was that now it bothered him. He had several bad dreams that he could not remember. He read all the news about Hatashil and it was all bad. But every morning, he ran.

Ten days before his flight home, Teak went to a dinner in Karen. At the high security gate he had to squint against the bright colors: green grass and blue jacaranda and purple bougainvillea. Inside, the white gravel crunched under Teak's shoes. He did not want to go to this dinner but he felt it was his job to put in an appearance. The parties were never more than panning for information. "Twice a decade, an agent," Lunt had said. Luxury was always a good cover. And perhaps it would make him forget the village for a while, Blackford and all that. He needed a distraction. The better he looked, Teak knew, the less he had to talk. He'd had one of his three identical suits cleaned the day before.

That morning he had read the lead Talk of the Town piece in the *New Yorker*. It was about the committee to investigate Susan Lowell's Hatashil book, and the possibility that, for the second time ever, a Pulitzer would be rescinded. Teak was also interested to learn that a Harvard undergrad had originally broken the whole Lowell-Hatashil mess in the American media, a *Crimson* reporter named Jane Baker. She was described in it as "looking like a young Cybill Shepherd." She had since done a television interview. Susan Lowell, meanwhile, had been inundated with requests for response but was keeping quiet.

How did that all get started? thought Teak. Now Lowell was fucked, too. Bad luck. At least she's not dead. No such thing as luck, though.

Ashamed to obey orders.

At the end of the white gravel drive a boy opened the second gate for Teak and led him to the front porch, where the hostess was talking on her cell phone. She snapped it shut when she saw Teak and said, "Michael, you must meet Jane." A colonially rough grand dame, fat in middle age, the hostess prided herself on getting to the point. "She's a Harvard girl, and she's more gorgeous than you are."

She took Teak's arm and led him through the house to French doors. They looked out over a very green lawn toward a fire pit where Milton Lambert drank heartily from a bottle of Tusker and tried to look down Jane Baker's sleeveless blouse.

Aesthetically, Teak and Jane were close to the ideals of each others' private school education. Both straightening their backs, they shook hands, and Teak caught himself admiring the smooth tone of Jane's thin arms.

"Isn't it something," said Jane, gestering at the musicians sitting on white chairs in a corner of the garden. "I've never heard a string quartet before."

Teak had. When he was in fifth grade in New York, he began attending the Knickerbockers School of Manners in a brownstone between Park and Madison Avenues. The lessons began on the first day with a slightly overweight old gentleman in a dinner jacket shaking the hand of each student and saying "How do you do, sir?" or "How do you do, miss?" The boys and the girls, seated in chairs on opposite sides of a grand ballroom, were called upon to rise, pair off in rotation, and learn to foxtrot, waltz, and cha-cha.

Teak had not liked Knickerbockers. On return from his first class he resolutely told his mother and father that he didn't need to be taught how to shake hands and that he would not be going back. Who needs to be taught how to shake hands? I already know how to shake hands! But his parents insisted. Teak was not given to tantrums but he argued and even shouted about Knickerbockers. His parents offered explanations. Though exasperated with Teak's stamina, they reasoned with him until his argument subsided. They never said "that's that," but neither did they relent. And in the end, Teak was tired, and he agreed that maybe it wasn't such a bad thing after all, and he went back. And after that, he liked it. He learned to foxtrot, and waltz, and cha-cha, and like everything else he practiced as a child, dancing became second nature to him.

By his senior year of college Teak had been to so many debutante balls, so many formals, he had forgotten that in the beginning he didn't like dancing. It was just something he did, dancing. The formals were as silly as the single beds and the foolish posters on the wall and the absolutely asinine comments people made on their Facebook profiles. But Teak had danced anyway, and enjoyed it all. It was absurd, but somehow, looking back on it, it was like his job, too.

* * *

"Dance with an old man?" Lambert asked Jane, setting his beer down on the edge of the fire pit.

"There's no one dancing."

"We'll make a spectacle of ourselves," insisted Lambert.

Jane laughed and took his outstretched hand. She looked over her shoulder at Teak, false alarm in her slightly parted lips and raised eyebrows. Teak cut in after a few minutes. Jane kissed Lambert on the cheek when he did. Teak lead her around the garden to the ¾, inspiring smiles and raised glasses at each knot of guests they passed.

"It's like Edith Wharton in Africa over here," commented Jane.

"I hope so," said Teak. He was enjoying the nonchalant delicacy of her hand on his shoulder. It hit him that he had forgotten how good it was to just want a pretty girl and he was relieved momentarily of the previous month and the slow corrosion it was working on him.

"Of course, there's the serious stuff, too." Jane wanted to let Teak know that she wasn't just a silly tourist. "Do you know about Hatashil?"

"You wrote the first story about Susan Lowell," said Teak.

"Oh God, you saw that? I think *he's* really the most interesting character. The committee is still investigating her research."

"You got some attention."

"For a week or so, yeah, that execution rumor. You know how these things spiral," Jane laughed. "Good for me, though. And really, maybe the truth will come out."

"The truth?" queried Teak.

The strings seemed to exhale as the music stopped. They turned because Milton Lambert was calling them. He demanded that they come and sit with him.

The three of them talked and eyed each other over the crystal and silver of the dinner. Teak was still thinking about Susan Lowell and Hatashil, but he didn't mention them. *Maybe later*. They talked right through the coffee and brandy, and Lambert switched back to Barolo and kept drinking. Teak and Jane didn't keep up with him, but they drank a great deal, too.

It was a perfect conversation. Jane said something outrageous, to which Teak responded thoughtfully and Lambert comically. Then Lambert said something outrageous, and Jane said something comic, and so on. She flirted with both of them. The cycle was entertaining, and they covered politics, wildlife, art, the hostess and her stuck up friends (here Teak was silent). Other guests, drawn to their beauty and heat, joined them at the table. Lambert welcomed the new blood and Jane noted the ease with which Teak chatted with each of them. She was always half listening to him even when she was talking with someone else.

Teak stood up to use the bathroom and clear his head. The first one he came to was occupied so he walked through the house to another, by the back garden. Though the musicians had packed away their instruments after appetizers, as Teak turned off the faucet he heard a sad, slow violin.

The music was coming from outside the back door, and Teak went to its window. He saw one of the musicians, sitting by himself in the empty back garden, playing slowly, looking drunk. As Teak listened and watched through the window screen he was startled by a hand on his shoulder.

Jane stood behind him, cocking her head.

"The music again," she said, and then, tipsy and thrilling herself, took Teak's hand to dance in the hallway to the single violin.

"This is all at the expense of the Africans," she said. "We are corrupt." Teak's shoulder under her hand reminded her of David's shoulder and she thought, *this is how it happens*. This could be the end of David. Because no matter how exotic Teak was, banging around Karen and in places beyond Jane's experience, Teak would never really be that different from her. He was glamorous but not alien. He would never be black. Jane had put in her time with David. Now she could relax. *Simple,* Jane thought, *I should just do what I want.*

"I went to dancing school," Teak said, struck by an erection and an idea at the same time. Perhaps that was it. Perhaps he had been obeying bullshit orders, from Knickerbockers on down the line. His job. He was passing all of his agents on, but if Jane could start the mess for Lowell and Hatashil, maybe she could do something to stop it. Maybe Teak could run her as an agent. His own private agent. An Independent Service for Information of two. It was a long shot that anything she did mattered anyway. But he wanted something to do, a project. *Better than talking to myself.*

The dance in the hallway was slower and shorter than in the garden and they bantered more because they were alone. Teak asked questions. When the music stopped Jane used the bathroom and Teak rejoined the party in the front garden, where he discovered the other guests had left or were leaving. The hostess stood by the fire pit, muttering something to one of the black waiters. The firelight flickered on her white skin, his black.

Lambert stood next to her and waved Teak over. He invited Teak to come with him for a nightcap.

"We have some mutual friends to discuss."

Before Teak could respond, Jane was with them, and Lambert invited her, too.

"I have some speakers for my iPod," she said, looking from Lambert to Teak and back. "We can all dance some more."

Teak nodded and rubbed the burn on his thumb against his index finger, as he had been doing all day.

38

Susan Lowell sat in her office after another long day of too few phone calls. She flipped to the next picture on her laptop, a candid shot of herself and Hatashil, neither of them looking at the camera. She was smiling in it, but she couldn't remember about what. He was brooding and looking at the ground, pointing at a drawing he had made in the dirt with his skull-topped cane. Susan tried to remember those days, remember some clue. About him, about herself. How she used to work so easily. She wondered if she could have missed the man's nature so fully. In the next picture they are shaking hands and smiling at each other. Now, she looked at his round belly, his frank stance. No. She was right. The world was full of shit. She was suddenly furious. She felt a momentary rage, like thorns blooming in her chest. She picked up the phone.

Susan had resisted calling Roger Knustle. She had, in fact, resisted finding him at the Cellar and punching him in the face. Now she called him, and got to the point.

"You told Razi that Hatashil's own people were killed," she said, "so where are you getting this "Hatashil's massacre" stuff?"

"One of my Delta sources said Hatashil did it himself," Knustle said. "He found a traitor in the village."

"Out of character."

"This is a source for my book."

"He would say whatever his bosses tell him to say."

"If he's lying about this, then he'd be lying about everything I'm writing my book about. I'm advanced and deadlined on all this. I'm sure of this guy."

Susan almost spit into the phone. "So you're right just because it's too hard to go back."

"Don't question *my* integrity." Knustle was infuriatingly calm. "You're still infatuated. He's like all the rest of them."

"Infatuated? Fuck off." Susan hung up. She did not feel any better. Maybe she should get that Jane Baker girl in for a meeting.

39

David had gotten it: the *final* invitation, to this *final* dinner, for admission into this *final* club. It specified that the bearer arrive on time and prepared to make a speech from memory. Robert had gotten the invitation, too, and David was unnerved by this. They were the only two foreigners left. David hoped they were not somehow linked in the eyes of the club members, but he feared they were.

"Good street," said Robert as they walked over the cobblestones that wet evening. The final dinner was to be held at a gentleman's club called the River Club, on Beacon Hill.

"I wonder who will be there," wondered David.

"Half the fockers who were there last time."

David wanted to ask Robert his feelings about the club, if he really wanted to get in or was just playing it off, as they said here. But he restrained himself, because he did not want to reveal how much *he* cared. The one time he had asked, Robert had snorted something about some Scottish fish. Or so David thought. He wasn't sure what Robert had said.

Then his phone rang. It was a number he didn't recognize.

"Hello?"

"David, Alan Green here."

David nearly dropped the phone shifting it to the other ear.

"I want to ask you to think something over, David. The Boston Africa Action Group is having a press conference and a panel discussion soon, and I thought you might like to take part." At his desk, Alan Green looked at a photo of Teak and his daughters on horseback as he spoke.

"I don't really know a lot about it all," said David.

Green adjusted the photo slightly.

"Well, think it over and then call me. For the record, I think you should do it."

Can't do that, thought David. *Why did Green have to call me and mess with me right now?* He tried to focus on the dinner.

The dinner passed in a blur of clinking glasses, scraping steak knives, rivers of red wine. The tradition was to deliver the speech as a toast, and the punches weighed their options. Pacing, timing, windows in the conversation. And the speeches that floated out of their mouths came from times so removed that the modern steak knives set on the table might have risen up and done battle if, being forged steel, they were resentful on behalf of all weapons that had come before.

Spencer was there. He, too, had made the cut. Robert caught his eye and made a blow-job gesture at him. Spencer decided that he would just make the first speech, damn it.

"Whoever does not have the stomach for this fight, let him depart," he began.

Robert rolled his eyes at David across the table. "Henry the Fifth," he said, "fockin' predictable." David ignored him and watched Spencer.

Spencer continued. "Give him money to speed his departure since we wish not to die in that man's company. Whoever lives past today and comes home safely will rouse himself every year on this day, show his neighbor his scars, and tell embellished stories of all their great feats of battle. These stories he will teach his son and from this day until the end of the world we shall be remembered. We few, we happy few, we band of brothers; for whoever has shed his blood with me shall be my brother. And those men afraid to go will think themselves lesser men as they hear of how we fought and died together."

When Spencer sat down, Robert rose. After suggesting that the previous speech suffered from the English's general "arseholeness" he recited "Mo Ghile Mear," even though it was Irish, because it was the only thing popping through the wine. He did not translate it for them but the table of faces grinned and applauded when he sat back down in his chair afterward.

"I think he just made up some gibberish," said Spencer to the guy next to him.

That's it, thought David. *Robert's done.* And then he felt he had to make his toast. He had thought about this a lot. He decided that the thing to do was recite, in English, a story from home. It was the only thing he knew by heart, and it was long and people at home always laughed at it. It was a creation story about a tortoise that goes up to heaven, and it was in a kind of verse. He knew it so well, thought David, that there was no way he could mess it up. It was from his father.

He delivered it perfectly and to great hoots of laughter. His blood tingled with relief and the blessed success and he couldn't stop smiling. For the rest of the dinner he had a very fine time, drank the wine and bullshitted with the members and punches. He'd spent a lot of time with them, this fall. They really were his friends, he thought.

After the dinner, as they were all getting up to go, there was a shout and a tussle in the doorway. Between shoulders, David saw Spencer stumbling up off the floor, a streak of blood from his lip. Robert stood over him, yelling for him to say that again, "yeh fockin cunt."

40

Teak followed Lambert's truck, which wove soddenly along the dark road back into the city center. The street lamps were bright and more frequent on this side of the city, but the darkness between each could seem like a curtain over a carjacking. Teak, slightly drunk himself, wasn't worrying about that, though. Running Jane would be a small project, but at least it was something, and it wasn't exactly disobeying orders. He could convince Jane of his version of Hatashil's massacre. He played out the scenarios. He would convince her, and then she would could go back and . . . And what? Write an op-ed? Renounce her previous pieces? What, he wondered slowly, was a single mind worth? Or a single newspaper for college kids? Or a single university. Smearing Lowell had been easy, and he knew it would be harder to clean her up, and as always, at high cost. A small untruth in his relationship with Jane, for a clearer note sounded back home. Teak did not like mulling, equivocating. He decided willfully. For whatever it was worth, he would send her back to describe the massacre as it happened. And it was an excuse to stick with her for a while.

His headlamps flashed over the men and women walking along the side of the road. It was a cold night, and Teak thought that the woman in a T-shirt he saw pushing a cart must be cold. It was hard to tell in the dark, but it looked like the cart was full of fruit. Mangoes looked just as yellow, green, and soft in the headlights as they did in the daylight.

When Lambert stopped in front of the Stanley, Teak stuck his head out the window and watched Jane's tipsy, elegant descent from the cab of the truck. A doorman in a red frock coat held the door for her. She tossed her pashmina over her shoulder and walked into the lobby. She must have decided to go to bed. He had thought that she would at least say good-bye. He'd just have to catch her again somehow.

Lambert was now forearming Teak's window, leaning in.

"You're going to leave me alone with her in her room for a nightcap?" Lambert winked at him.

Jane's minibar had only two Tuskers. Room service wasn't operating anymore and the bar downstairs was closed. Lambert said he would have more beers in no time and left Teak and Jane alone.

"Why do you like me?" Jane asked Teak as soon as Lambert was out the door.

"Who said I like you?"

He kissed her. They kissed.

* * *

And suddenly Lambert was back, with twelve Tuskers. Apparently he knew someone in the kitchen.

"Do you want it cold," Lambert said as a joke to Teak. Jane wouldn't get it, Teak thought, that the only beer in Africa that wasn't warm was served on safari. But then she surprised him.

"I'm not on safari yet," she said, and went on to explain the weekend safari that she and her parents were taking. They were flying down to the Masai Mara.

"Better than Ngorongoro," said Lambert. "Fucking zoos, all of them, now."

"What a great date," said Jane.

"It's all dying," said Lambert, world-weary, tapping the window and the relative darkness of Nairobi outside. "Like your man here. A dying breed."

"He looks healthy to me," quipped Jane.

"Oh, he's dying," said Lambert, "it's not fun around here anymore."

Jane lay back on her bed. The room was spinning. *I'm cheating on David,* she thought. And the end of fun in Africa is a cliché. She lit a cigarette and blew the smoke up at the slowly turning fan. Lambert looked from her to Teak and laughed.

"Teak," she said, still lying on her back, "would you like to come with me and my parents up to the Masai Mara? I'm serious. You should. I'm drunk but I'm serious," she repeated, feeling carried away, like if she'd come this far . . . "You know, white horses on black backgrounds." She would not let Teak stay here tonight though, she thought.

Teak looked at her closely. "I'll think about it," he said. If north was up and south was down, he thought, then she meant for him to come down with her. But somehow he found her lack of orientation endearing. The innocence of it. Jane's eyelids were falling unevenly. Very drunk, thought Teak, too drunk. He was suddenly tired. "Thank you, Jane," he said, looking from Jane on the bed to Lambert, "it's late."

"Thanks for coming, boys," said Jane, closing her eyes.

Jane made no effort to take off her clothes. She realized as the door closed that she had to vomit. She knelt before the toilet. The red wine diffused in the water over the white porcelain. Sometimes, she thought, as she staggered to her bed, wiping her mouth, you had to drink. It was worth it to have spent the time with Teak, and even Lambert. It was the only way you could get close to people. She passed out, face down, in her shoes, on top of the covers, before she could think of Teak again.

41

The afternoon after the final dinner, David was angry and still hungover, searching for another John Stuart Mill book in the purgatorial fluorescent light of the library stacks. Maybe he should call Green and do the press conference. Maybe it would help him with the club. Robert had fucked up so badly and David figured it had definitely rubbed off on him.

But Hatashil wasn't an evil man. And it would be a betrayal of Professor Lowell and all those essays she had helped him with. He had been so grateful to her. Because it had been so hard in the beginning, when he had just arrived. She had been a friend, of sorts. And you needed friends here.

When he learned he had been accepted to Harvard, David was elated. But the elation quickly mingled with a kind of dread. His father, who had been to London once, talked to him about what it would be like in Boston. He described the way a lot of people, when they first went "over there," were so overwhelmed they stopped thinking. Some of them, he said, were so confused and embarrassed that they pretended it was all disappointing. That wasn't how he wanted David to be. David should find his own path. He must appreciate everything and he must be polite to everyone no matter how strange it all seemed. Above all, he must be alert, because he could learn much that he could bring home with him. And don't worry, his father said at the end of the talk, you will always come home.

David stopped believing he would go home at the end of the first year, about the time he began dating Jane. His father was right about the beginning, though. David's ride on the airplane was his first test. He was alert the whole time so that when he was landing in Heathrow he was tired but pleased with himself. It was easy. Everyone else had gone to sleep but he had stayed awake looking out the window and thinking about how high and fast it all was, even though it felt so slow. But then no one got off at Heathrow. David had not really understood about the stop and had not thought to ask anyone. When he realized he was not getting off the plane he was disappointed in himself and anxious.

When he finally landed at Logan he was determined not to be a fool. He picked up his bag from the carousel and went to find the subway to Harvard. Outside the airport he was struck by the immense parking lot he saw as he looked for the entrance to the subway. He liked it and wanted to stand in it among all those cars. It was like something from the movies he had seen, where travelers stood in the empty, perfect lot and talked about what to do next. He didn't stand there, of course, the important thing was to get to Harvard as quickly as possible.

It turned out that public transportation was the easy part; looking out the window of the T was great, rushing over the river past the huge skyscrapers, with somewhere to go. It was hard to imagine that the buildings hadn't always been there. The small concrete houses he knew so well, even the nicer, painted two-story ones like his father's, they all felt so constructed, so temporary by comparison. Even the big colonial school. Even Nairobi.

Harvard took him through the first day with a group of other international students. A short tour, getting into the dorm, key cards issued. But then they all seemed to split off in little groups that first night. David, to his great consternation, did not manage to join a group.

He went back to his empty room. The regular students, among them his roommate, would not arrive for another week. His fears returned. He was particularly unnerved by not knowing where he was. What would he do in the vastness of America when he didn't even know where he was? He went to sleep worried that he had made a big mistake. It was so fast to come, couldn't he just get back on the plane and go back? It wouldn't even have taken two days. He waited for the night to pass so he could have something to do again. Breakfast. That first night passed very slowly.

The next day was better. Harvard got easier the more he walked around, and soon he made friends. The university cradled him with ice-cream mixers and introductory meetings, activity fairs and a tour of Boston. David hid his amazement at the John Hancock building on the tour. But he was alert. The same thing for the Boston Common. It struck him as funny that real birds should be there, because the land was all so fake. He was especially amused by the brass ducks walking in a row that tourists photographed. Little statues in the middle of nowhere—of ducks.

There were some people he could joke with about it all. He had three countrymen at Harvard. He recognized in them some of what his father said. They acted like this place was no big deal. They were obsessed with technology and were showing off their phones. None of them were from as poor or as remote a place as he was, though, and there was that between them.

No big deal, that's what one of them said, over and over. The library is no big deal. What's a big deal is the project to take it all digital. But the library, in those early days, seemed to watch David wherever he walked across the Yard. It was so huge. He couldn't bring himself to go inside, though he wanted to very much and get all the books he needed for the semester. But no one had told him how it worked yet, and he didn't want to barge in. One of his countrymen told him that you got school books at a place called the Coop, so he went there in those first days, even though everyone said that classes didn't begin for another month, really not until the end of October. At the Coop he saw a few students walking out with great plastic bags of books. Then he overhead some of them talking about it and left right away—they had been talking about how they were spending seven hundred dollars on books that semester. When he finally went to the library he was embarrassed that he had ever been nervous about it. And it was like that for so many things he couldn't remember them all.

He remembered certain incidents very well, however. Like his first discussion section. He had a little bag that his mother had brought home from market one day, from the vast nebula of global discards and second-rates and hand-me-downs that end up in Africa. The toothpaste logo Crest was on it, and he had kept his pens and pencils in it all through high school. And at the end of section this girl had said to her friend something about how the bag was *really* vintage. It stung later, when David got it. After he met Jane.

That was when things started to change. He had started the year by joining every one of the African clubs. There was drumming. He had never before been interested in drumming but so many people did it that he did, too. Likewise for politics and African languages. He was surprised at how infrequently he ate with the white kids. He ate all his meals at the same table, with black kids. Not always Africans. American black kids, too. And for the beginning of that first year he was happy for the company. But as the year went on it started to bother him. He didn't know why exactly. But he knew fast that he liked lunch with Jane better than lunch at the African languages table.

David's phone rang, irritating his hangover. It was his father. Phone conversations with his father were rare. To talk across the ocean was expensive. David was surprised when he saw the long string of numbers—it was late over there—and it momentarily dissipated his anguish over what had happened at the dinner. The connection, as always, was distant, scratchy, and delayed. He had to pause before he spoke. He had discovered this when he had arrived and talked to his father over the phone that first time. If he spoke too soon after his father finished, the words were lost. This time he had no words.

On this call, his father told him that his cousins in the village had all been killed. And his aunt, "my sister," said his father slowly. David paused when his father finished but found he could not talk. The stacks around him, the millions of volumes, seemed as alien and ominous as they did that first week.

Finally, David asked his father who had killed his cousins. He could hear the great rage and sadness in his father's voice even through the scratchy and huge cellular distance between them.

"No one survived to tell."

David waited.

"All the newspapers, the white newspapers, too, are saying it was Hatashil's massacre."

42

"If you're a foreigner, your reason to be here expires and then . . ." Lambert trailed off and lit a cigar in the bay of his Chinook 414.

He and Teak sat on crates in the corrugated metal darkness. After leaving Jane, they had driven to the airport. Lambert said he liked to have a drink in one or another of his helicopters sometimes, before he went to bed. He owned three. He had greeted a guard at a side gate with a warm laugh and hand clasp, given him a cigarette, and the guy had let them through to the private hangars. *Big chopper,* thought Teak, *rich Lambert. He was either a very bad pilot or a very good one*. They were passing a flask of whiskey back and forth now.

"Like I told your girl, it used to be more fun," said Lambert. "Your people are incompetent, and let me tell you, the locals were never any good."

Alarm bells sounded in Teak's head. *Your people?* He was drunk again, and after the binge in his bedroom he had made a deal with himself. What was Lambert talking about? *Shit*. Teak didn't like him coming out and saying this, even though the rule he always worked by was that everybody knew what his real job was. *Reverse psychological flak jacket. Everybody knows who you are, even when you don't,* he thought, blinking heavily. He shook himself. He had to keep up with Lambert. And not talk much.

"This is the worst place now," Lambert went on. "It's like Hatashil, or Aziz Al-Emudi or whatever his real bloody name is, you think he'd stick around if he could go back to Saudi Arabia or Dubai and sit by the pool? That's why he has an exit base in Brava, on the coast. Lunt told me. You know. He stole millions, he could have been the head of DMI, and they want him dead. He's not here on jihad, he's hiding out. The reason you all like him is because he doesn't believe in anything, right?"

Teak nodded. Silence, silence, and too drunk to play any which way anyway. But he'd heard something like this before and it sobered him a little. Nothing worked if Hatashil was not the homegrown orphan revolutionary. Nothing worked if Hatashil didn't match the myth that suddenly seemed to have been so carefully created. *The myth that I,* thought Teak, *helped create.*

"But I like it here . . ." Lambert went on, flicking his cigar out the bay door into the darkness. "And I like giving people rides."

"Over the border?" Teak asked.

Making it home just before dawn, Teak was surprised to find an envelope on his bed. His door had been locked. It took him a moment, through the booze, to understand. Obviously someone had come in and placed it there. They must have gotten a key. He stood at the edge of his bed, frozen, for a long moment, looking at the envelope on his pillow, white and sealed.

Teak backed away from the bed and checked the bathroom, the kitchen. Only then did he return to the bedroom and open the envelope with his folding knife. Inside there was half a newspaper clipping: "U.S. Security Czar Applauds . . ."

The rest was ripped away. Handwritten under the headline in black ink, in block capitals, was a latitude and longitude, a date the following week, and the words: YOU ALONE.

43

Razi's phone, clock, and television all went off at once, ringing, beeping, and blaring together in shrill techno misery. The night before, Razi had set all the alarms to make sure he would wake up, which he did, with the familiar dry scratch in the back of his throat. The familiar headache. He had a cold that seemed never to leave his sinuses. But at least he was up. He lit a cigarette and smoked it as he shaved, looking at himself in the mirror. He was going to breakfast with Susan. He had suggested drinks, but she wanted breakfast. She got her way, as usual.

As he was shaving, his phone rang again. Razi cut himself, swore, and in so doing spat his cigarette into the sink where the ash mingled with his whiskers. As he held his phone to his lathered face he imagined that it might short out and that he would live the rest of his life with a cellphone-shaped burn on his face.

"Razi? It's Bill."

Bill Bester had been a classmate at Georgetown. He worked for the *Washington Post*. Razi had always liked him, though occasionally he was irritated by Bill's high polish. His business cards, for example, were on surprisingly heavy paper, special ordered. They had been doing each other favors since they had split lecture notes in American democracy. Razi carried one of Bester's business cards in his wallet.

"I woke you up," he said.

It irritated Razi when people assumed they had woken him up, as if he was always sleeping in. He was even more irritated when he rolled over in semisleep and picked up the phone and it was impossible to pretend that he had been awake and not sleeping in his shoes. He looked over to the corner of the room where his shoes and socks lay irregularly, kicked off just before unconsciousness.

"I think you might want to check out today's *LA Times*."

"Oscar preview?"

"Remember your friend Marina?"

Of course, but Razi had met her only once, with Susan. Toma had pointed her out, sitting at the bar at the Peponi hotel, when the three of them had all taken a week in Lamu to swim in the sea. Susan had insisted that Toma come and paid for his trip. Marina had also come to relax, having just completed a stressful deal in Congo in which one of her admittedly old planes had failed take off after it had delivered defective ammunition. The customer's sergeant had registered his anger on the pilot with the stock of his Kalishnikov. Marina was enjoying the hot solitude and was surprised when Susan introduced herself at the bar.

Susan was graceful as she explained her book and after some small talk she politely agreed with Marina that it was better for them not to talk about work. After that was out of the way, they had all hit it off and spent the night drinking strong, sweet "Old Pals," the hotel's house drink. Razi had always wanted to write about Marina, but except for that one time at the bar Marina remained a rumor. It was hard to prove her name, never mind that she was an arms dealer and that the United States allowed, and even encouraged, her in her business. Razi thought it was incredible luck that Toma had recognized her at all. He said he had seen her once with one of Hatashil's lieutenants. But then, Toma was always lucky about Hatashil. Susan took it for granted sometimes. *So did I,* thought Razi.

"What about Marina?" said Razi into the phone.

"The ATF and FBI arrested her in Miami and had a joint press conference."

"*Miami?*"

"Apparently she found a new market, some kind of Chavez-inspired anti-American militia."

"A what? To do what? Retake Texas?"

"That was the joint statement."

Razi thought about Director Harrison's sudden change of policy. "Guess she was in the wrong place at the wrong time . . ." he trailed off, waiting for Bill to finish.

"Or maybe they'd just been planning to nail her from the beginning."

But that is a shitty theory, thought Razi after he hung up. Bester was well connected but his theories were always off. Razi was sure that Marina had helped the United States with Hatashil and that's why they had left her alone. Better for her to arm Hatashil than do it themselves. Ship a single round and the whole world screams Iran Contra again. Razi looked forward to telling Susan. It was more evidence that somebody was systematically going after Hatashil. They could work on connecting the dots. Maybe he could help her.

This is what Razi was still thinking when he walked into Upstairs on the Square, late for breakfast. Susan looked even better than usual to Razi, as though her good looks extended to everything around her. The steam from her tea caught the sunlight. The sunlight refracted through her orange juice. Her hair was just so.

Since her integrity had been called into question, Susan had been even more careful than usual about putting herself together. Her nerves and doubts had manifested themselves in new shoes, extra attention to makeup. She only wished that she could clean up her work somehow, but all she did was make phone calls. Which felt meaningless. She spiraled if she wasn't careful about her clothes. She knew what she ought to do was go and see for herself, find Hatashil again. But she wasn't going to do that. It just seemed like a hassle, and she was disgusted with herself for feeling that way. Her colleagues were wary of her, her students suspicious. The worst was when old friends called to offer their support. She hated that, even though she knew she shouldn't. And Harry was overly protective. The balance of her marriage was off. Usually the marriage worked because she and Harry left each other alone. But with Susan so clearly—and publicly—suffering, Harry had been trying to do too much for her. He kept asking her if she "was all right." It pissed her off and saddened her at once. It was important to look good, at least. *Razi,* she thought as he approached, *did not.* But at least he was always there for her.

Razi was about to tell her his news but she spoke first.

"Our friend Marina was arrested yesterday," Susan told him as he sat down. "In Miami, of all places."

Razi resisted the urge to order a Bloody Mary.

"The Agency will never work with her again, obviously," Susan folded up her paper and put it to the side of her fruit salad. "And they've made an enemy of her, too, if she ever gets out."

"Which she will," said Razi.

When Susan left to teach her human rights class, he ordered his first drink of the day.

44

Had it been a different day, a different quarter to eleven, perhaps ten years earlier, Jane would have heard a great explosion. She would have looked up suddenly, her brown eyes wide with surprise, heard without knowing the low patterns of nearby death. If Teak had been with her, he probably would have run from the café, straight along Kimathi Street, left on Mama Ngina, and right on Moi, where he would have seen the wreckage at the American embassy.

But this day in the Thorn Tree Café Jane did not hear an explosion. There was only the café chatter. She was trying to compose an e-mail to Teak. It was difficult but it was a delicious difficulty, as she might say. She was stuck on salutations. "Teak," "Dear Teak," "M," "Hey," "Yo," She giggled when she wrote "Yo."

She hadn't felt like this in a long time, or what for her was a long time. Definitely not since nine months ago when she met David. But there was a difference. She knew she could have David. In that relationship she was in a position of power. Something she did not feel with Teak. She wished Teak would call and pick her up and take her to bed. She wished she could pick him up and take him to bed. She just didn't know what to write in the e-mail. Maybe the trick was to be honest, to tell him that whenever he wanted he could call her and she would want him. Or maybe that was too passive, she had to write that she wanted him, as soon as possible. But that was the whole problem. None of this was right. *Don't I have to be cool,* she wondered, *write nothing, not care*. That would make me the most attractive to him. But is not writing the e-mail the same as not caring?

Jane knew the answer to that. Maybe she could just write the e-mail and not spell it all out. What private joke could she begin with, what had they spoken of? She looked at her phone as the Gikuyu waiter brought her latte. The waiter paused for a moment, putting down the drink. The girl had a glow. Maybe she was newly pregnant. The waiter was glad he had read some Psalms that morning. He had a lot of tables just then but he wanted to sneak out to top up his cell phone at the supermarket across the street. He had to call his little brother, who was about to become a father for the first time.

As she drank her second latte, Jane wondered when Teak would come back to the United States. It was inconceivable to her that he would not return one day. It was simple, really. Why wouldn't you want to live among your family, where everything worked, where the lattes were better? Teak would come home, and they would have a relationship. Maybe he was someone she could marry.

She had thought about marriage more when she was a little girl than when she was in college. When she was little she had tea parties in the drawing room of the house in Beacon Hill. She had memories of the long curtains that she would open a sliver, piercing her mother's drawing room with the light from over the river. She had sat on the floor, with her own tea set, and talked to her imaginary husband. They talked about private schools.

But then in high school, when she first started kissing boys, she realized that she would not be married for a long time. The reason was simple. She had to find the perfect man. After all, this was the biggest decision of her life. Jane knew her biology. This was the whole point. If you had brilliant, beautiful parents, more likely than not you were brilliant and beautiful. And people wondered why the adopted kids, those children of peasants in Tigray or Hunan, magically transported to the Upper East Side, tended to get in so much more trouble, spend so much more time in rehab. Thinking about, she felt a strong and sudden urge, an ache, to cradle a child in her arms.

Teak might be good enough, she thought. She still had not written a word of the e-mail, but a bold idea fell through her mind. She set her latte aside and deleted his address from the "to" field, in case she accidentally hit send, and started to write. She wrote that she was in love with him and that he might actually be the one, she could see them getting married and having children, but not of course until they had had enough adventures of their own. And why shouldn't they just go for broke right then? She tested it out, typing the words.

But then, as though volunteering a confidence at a cocktail party, Jane felt the small but ragged shame of betrayal. She thought of David, even though she knew that she had to put herself first because *that was what life is about, right?*

She thought of his face. She pictured what his eyes and wide mouth would do when she told him in person that there was someone else. And then she noticed, in the corner of the café, her waiter with a cell phone to his ear pumping his fist in the air. David would be fine, she decided. After all, he wouldn't end up back in Africa.

45

It had rained all night. David hurried along one of the wet stone paths crossing Harvard Yard. He wanted to check his mailbox between classes, for the internships. *Dead cousins*. The internship led to the real job after college, the path. He had been alternately numb and wired since his father's phone call. It *had* been Hatashil. And his girlfriend had broken the story. She was always right, he thought. And he never was. Even about the great Professor Lowell, whom he had trusted. He would listen to Jane from now on. He saw a pair of her friends sitting close together on the steps of the library, smoking in the cold, their long soft coats draped around them.

And he would work harder, just study, and somehow get an internship. Because after Robert had behaved so badly he was sure neither of them would make the club. No new connections. It made him grind his teeth. He had been avoiding Robert. He walked fast everywhere. *Dead cousins. No job. I'll have to go home.*

* * *

That damp day Robert found him. They stood, face to face, in front of the steps of Memorial Church, dedicated to the memory of those who gave their lives in the Great War. "He called yeh a nigger," Robert said.

David tried to walk around him but Robert caught him by the arm.

"He was making some crack about how it was a nigger song from the dark continent."

David slapped his arm away. "You screwed us."

"I can't believe what the fock I'm hearing."

"I can't believe you had to drag me into it."

"Drag you into it? I was fockin' defending you."

"I don't need to be defended," David yelled.

"What's your fockin problem?"

"Nothing," said David. *Nothing*. "You're the problem."

"Fock yourself."

They walked off in separate directions. David consoled himself: Robert was a drunk, and there had been a drunk in his town and this drunk appeared in his mind now. The drunk was an old man, and he sat on the main road from morning to night, drinking whatever he could get. The road was the only place aside from the colonial school where you might see a *mzungu* out walking, and the drunk liked to call out to *wazungu* if they passed. He always said the same thing: "*bon soir, mzungu!*" no matter the time of the day, no matter that *bon soir* was the only French he spoke, no matter that the *wazungu* were all British or Italian. He must have thought it funny. If a drunk did that here the cops would take him away. But no one would take

Robert away, David thought darkly. He's not the nigger. *Another reason I need to get into that club, another reason he screwed me. Dead cousins.*

David's thoughts spun into each other as he walked into the mailroom of his dorm. He dialed his combination lock three times before he got it right. He had received no offers for internships, just two flyers. One from a new all-night mental health office in the basement of a freshman dorm. The other was an invitation to the next Boston Africa Action Group open meeting.

He took out his phone and looked at Alan Green's phone number.

46

The moment Teak woke up he remembered the envelope. His bed faced east and the rising sun brought an acidic sweat out on his forehead. He pushed himself out of bed. The night was blurry, although he remembered parts of it vividly. The softness of Jane's lips. Other parts were vague, something Lambert had said, *important*. He couldn't remember. But it would come back. It always did. He took a cold shower but all it did was make him cold.

He looked at the bags under his eyes in the mirror as he shaved. The newspaper clipping with the coordinates was unfolded on the toilet cistern next to the sink. He glanced at it as he lathered his face. He had not yet decided what to do about it. Certainly nothing until his hangover was gone.

Rubbing on aftershave he had brought months ago from New York, he thought of Jane and whether he would go to the Masai Mara with her. He hadn't decided about that yet either. He imagined one of those lodges with the tourists lined up for breakfast, and then lined up to be driven around, and then lined up for gin and tonics after the game ride. He saw himself meeting Jane's parents in the big hall by the fireplace where the Danes would be comparing binoculars. And then he imagined coming in Jane, in one of the bedrooms. The window would look out over a stand of fever trees and the only creatures that would see them making love would be the greedy marabous with their plundering beaks. The beaks were long, and sharp enough to pierce the hide of a rhino. The other carrion eaters of the Mara, and places like it, followed the marabou because they opened the carcass, penetrated it first so the others could dig in. The marabou's beak going, in and out, up to its neck, and the dumb, vicious eyes. Teak thought about sex. *Dumb and vicious.*

And, of course, he would talk to Jane about Lowell and Hatashil again. He picked up the paper with the coordinates, folded it, and tucked it into the pocket of his jacket.

Outside his door the traffic and dust of the city blasted him. He put on his sunglasses and walked slowly, focusing on the sunshine on his skin and trying to breathe slowly, willing the traffic into silence. He would eat something. He would avoid the traffic, survive the walk to work another day.

What was it that Lambert had said? Something about a base, a particular place? An exit? He clenched his teeth, angry with himself. *Off the case.*

He should call Lunt. He should report the clipping in his pocket, the coordinates. Instead, he called Jane's hotel. When he was connected he said that, yes, he would love to join her and her parents on safari.

47

"I want to talk at the conference," said David. "I would like to tell everyone that Susan Lowell is very wrong."

"Good man," said Alan Green. "These small things, these bricks, that's how you make a difference."

After they hung up David went back to his room. He had a meeting scheduled with Lowell, but to hell with her. He was skipping it. He had never done that before. He didn't want to see the woman who turned Hatashil into a hero. *Cousins.* She probably wouldn't even notice, he thought. Instead of going to the meeting, he lay on his bed looking at the Harvard shield on his planner, thinking of the day he had given the Harvard mugs to all his cousins.

He was looking forward to Jane's return. He wanted her righteous rage, though he had disliked it in her before. He wanted it turned on Professor Lowell, shared with him. The anger would be more satisfying shared. He tried to imagine what Jane would say about it all. She'd probably tell him to drop the course. She'd say Lowell was corrupt or "incapable of understanding because she was American," or something like that. He couldn't imagine saying that, but he knew Jane could. And she could convince him of it, too. She would say he was doing the right thing. Most importantly, she'd say making the speech was a great idea.

And then there was the club. Jane could mock all she wanted but she understood why it was important, how it was connected to everything else. She was part of it herself. He wanted her to reassure him of that. He imagined telling her that he had gotten in, and what her reaction would be, and the look on her face.

48

On the small plane, meeting the guides, laughing at first about the giraffes, they were comfortable together as a couple, alone and in a group on safari. Jane's parents mostly left them alone, spent their time talking with their own friends. Each night, Teak and Jane stayed up late talking about their families and the small but crucial embarrassments and axles of their childhoods. They revealed themselves quickly, like travelers. They spoke, too, about nature, had their private jokes about monkeys and sex. And about the people on the trip. They did not discuss whole swaths of their lives, but the full revelation of certain aspects of character and history bonded them in isolation. Teak knew this phenomenon from his short years of solitary travel and life abroad. Jane had never encountered it before and she fell fully into it, even the possibility that it could be the same somewhere else as it was here, over coffee in a silver pot, under the bright stars of the Masai Mara. They fucked late into the night.

The fifth morning of the trip Teak awoke to the looping call of a ring-necked dove. Jane breathed easily next to him in the coming heat. One of the boys softly called hello from outside the tent flap and Jane stirred. Teak stepped quietly out of the bed and sat in a canvas chair. Jane awoke as Teak took the silver tray of tea from the *boy* and laid it on the table next to the bed.

"They want us up to look for that leopard again don't they," said Jane from the pillow.

Teak nodded as he sipped his tea.

"Let's not obey orders this morning," said Jane. "I mean, what's the point of all this? We should just do what we want to do."

Teak looked at her.

"Pass me the sugar," she said.

Teak took the sugar off the tray and sat on the bed next to her.

"I've been meaning to tell you," he said.

She sat up and looked at him, taking the sugar.

"Hatahsil's massacre," he began. "I was there."

He told her that he had been up there on business for the Fund, and that he had seen the whole thing. Hatashil did not commit a massacre, someone had tried to assassinate him. He did not suggest that she change her story before she said, "I have to get the word out."

Right, thought Teak. And as soon as she said it he was disappointed, because he knew it probably wouldn't mean anything. He considered confessing who he really was but confessed nothing. He was impressed at how determined she was to bear her responsibility, even if it was only bad journalism.

"I don't do drugs, you know," Jane said. "We weren't talking about it but I thought you'd like to know.

He nodded, and she was sure that she wanted him to know exactly who she was.

After they fucked and lazed in bed for a while, Jane fell asleep again. Teak rose. From the inner pocket of his tan jacket he took the newspaper clipping with the coordinates and his phone. He stepped outside and walked to the base of a fever tree. He looked at the coordinates on the note and called Milton Lambert to ask if he could catch a ride in a few days.

49

Robert stood in front of his mailbox in Quincy house. He held in his hand a letter from the administrative board. The ad board, as it was popularly known, was responsible for disciplinary action against students. Spencer had reported Robert on charges of assault.

The letter required Robert to go before the board, composed of a mix of students and faculty, to explain himself. Spencer would do the same. Robert's advocate in the process was to be his senior tutor. Robert didn't know the guy at all, but he knew he was an enthusiastic leader of house community spirit. Robert remembered the senior tutor's plastic, saccharine smile and the way he had cried at last year's commencement. *What a fuckhead,* thought Robert. On the verge of a loss, the real disintegration of a friendship, Robert allowed himself the relief of anger in all directions.

He walked to Felipé's for a burrito. He didn't want to have lunch in the dining hall. The ambitious glances, the small talk. The shit food. He would have a burrito instead and think on what to do about this assault charge. He wasn't sure but he thought there was a two-strike policy. So he wouldn't be expelled. Strike one, though. He had indeed punched Spencer to the ground. For all the talk of what it meant to be black on campus Robert suspected that no one would see the situation as he did. That is, that the *wee racist focker had it comin'*.

50

Teak listened to Lambert through the headset buzz of the helicopter and looked out at the sky rather than down at the earth.

"Did you go on safari with the girl?" asked Lambert.

"Masai Mara," said Teak.

"How was she," asked Lambert. He looked at Teak and grinned. Teak said nothing and touched his knuckles to the warm glass of the cockpit, blocking the yellow sun from view. The ride had saved him four days on dangerous roads. Lambert had a contract to lift some USAID people out of Mandera, and Teak was an easy drop-off on the way.

When he landed, Teak checked in on the Wildlife Fund's satellite office. A fan rotated over a pair of biologists at an old metal table. They leaned over a laptop, entering ibis sightings into a spreadsheet. They were very happy to see Teak. He told them he was up to see how the office was getting on, but really just wanted a reason to get out of the city for a few days. Maybe take a drive and camp overnight somewhere. He took one of their trucks and drove to a smaller town nearby.

The coordinates were for a café. Teak drove by, parked, scanned the road, and walked back. A small boy jumped back and forth over the sewage gutter. A green and white hand-painted sign—"Star Buck's"—hung from the thatch over the three tables. Toma was sitting at one of them, his eyes shaded by a plain black baseball cap. Though it was hot, he wore a canvas jacket and kept one hand in a pocket. Teak sat down and ordered a Mirinda.

"Hello, Toma," said Teak. He hoped his surprise didn't show.

Toma looked at Teak with wide, intense eyes. "You know what you all call me?"

"What do you mean?"

"The name journalists and you have for me."

A "fixer," said Teak. He didn't like where this was going.

The waiter came and asked Toma what he would like. "Chai," Toma said. Then to Teak, "someone has asked me to fix you."

Toma took a black cell phone from his pocket and put it on the table between them. Teak recognized the phone. He had given it to Hatashil. It was at that moment that Teak understood about Toma. *Of course.*

"I did not believe," said Toma, "that you would betray someone that way."

"I didn't," said Teak. "How long have you been working for him?"

Toma ignored the question. "I also believed that you would come here today, and you did." Toma smiled; amused, toothy, yellow. "Did you know the attack was coming?"

"No," said Teak.

Toma bummed a cigarette from Teak, lit it, blew the smoke skyward. "I like fixing," he said. "Being a soldier is just the business of killing people and destroying things."

"Of course," said Teak.

"The best job I ever did was working for Susan Lowell."

"I read the book."

"Everyone read the book. She still doesn't know I'm with him." Toma chuckled, remembering, and then said, "he is a brilliant man."

Toma blew cigarette smoke on his tea and sipped it. Teak thought, momentarily, about the specificity of blowing on tea, how it was a gesture that all men, all over the world, had in common.

"The belief," said Toma, "is that you confirmed his presence and then called in your friends."

"It wasn't us."

Toma stubbed out his cigarette with one hand, his other still in his pocket. "Who, then? China? The Brits? Executive Outcomes? The Pentagon? You all work together."

"We're supposed to."

Toma laughed a dry, unhappy laugh. "I believe you."

Teak heard the click of a pistol hammer in Toma's pocket.

51

"I think I'll get a convertible myself," said Willy. The day was bright and Lucas and Willy were in high spirits. Lucas had discovered Zipcar. By registering on the Web site he was able to pick up any of a number of cars parked around Boston and for an hourly rate drive it wherever he pleased. He and Lucas, tuxedoed as usual, had been driving laps around campus and waving to people out the window. No one drove, so they were getting a lot of attention in their convertible red Mini Cooper with the top down. Which was how they liked it.

They saw Razi walking up Garden Street and slowed. Willy shouted at him. "Hallo, fellow barfly."

Razi nodded at them and continued walking. Willy persisted. "Barfly, we are of the same tribe, can we offer you a ride, perhaps to the Cellar?"

At another time, Razi thought, he would have known just what to say back to the little fucker. But he only nodded at them again and vowed to call back the Emudi source he'd ignored.

What am I doing anyway, he thought. He was just walking around, waiting for the evening.

"Come on then, professor," said Willy.

"Fuck off," called Razi as they sped away, making himself feeling lame.

Willy didn't hear and over his shoulder he called out. "See you at the bar."

52

On his belly on the roof across the street, Moalana watched Teak and Toma. He recognized Teak. The goofy *mzungu* with the suitcases of *khat*. Funny orders, he thought.

Moalana had been a boy when he was conscripted into Hatashil's brigade, though it was not really a conscription. He had wanted to join—he was thirteen. There had been a drought. One of the last good wells had been given to a newcomer, from the capital, and he didn't allow anyone on his property, though Moalana's father had been watering his stock there for a long time. Moalana's father was reluctant to go farther south, though there was greater promise, because he wished to live where his father had lived. With the death and consumption of his family's final cow, they had moved to the nearest town. The hope was that he might earn enough money, one day, to buy another cow and start again. This was humiliating for the old nomad, but Moalana's father was a practical man. Whenever the aid planes came through and the *mzungus* distributed grain, he kept some and sold some in this hope, and his wife did the same, and they ate less, but they had hope.

Moalana did not go to school so he hung around the airstrip. Once he made a miraculous five American dollars carrying luggage for some people on safari, which he used to by the finest knockoff trainers in the market. There was no other pair like them, and he wore them proudly as he acted as a porter and assistant to a *mzungu* girl who worked in a small aid office. He used to buy cigarettes and fruit for her and load her truck. He swept the office sometimes. He never liked the work, but she paid him. Not like the housekeeper her mother had back in Oregon, more like fifteen dollars a month, for Moalana, at thirteen. But then the *mzungu* girl had left and he had almost no money.

Then, hanging around the airstrip one day, an older boy had invited him to a secret meeting. He went. He got drunk for the first time, with a couple older boys who were in town to shop. That was what impressed Moalana, that these boys had money to buy a lot of things all at once. "Supplies," they said. They enlisted Moalana to watch for the NSF while they went to the market. This was about the time his father and mother had finally saved almost enough money to purchase a cow, and they were planning on leaving town soon. The third time Moalana was asked by the older boys to watch, he saved them from detection when he saw NSF soldiers arriving to shakedown the shop. The older boys fled out the back and, pleased with Moalana, shared a beer with him later that day. On impulse Moalana asked to leave with them right then. They brought him out into the bush where they all slept on mats under a tall, gnarled acacia tree.

The homesickness, the longing for his parents that he felt that night, was worse than anything he had ever known. He couldn't just leave the camp, but he resolved that on the next supply run he would return to his parents. The next run was not for a long time, though, and then Moalana nearly wept when he was told he could not go on it. Finally, he was allowed to go back to town, finally a break from the ceaseless drinking and apparently aimless marching exercises and driving around in the wilderness, from village to village, wherever someone had a sympathetic cousin, maybe, and something to eat. All for Hatashil —father, teacher, sword at the throat of the NSF. This did not make sense to Moalana, but he was stuck.

Finally back in town, Moalana could not find his parents. They were gone; dead, or maybe they had managed to buy the cow and leave, or Moalana didn't know what. Thirteen was practically a man, he said to himself, of course they would not wait for me. But how could they not wait? He kicked up the dust in front of the Oregonian *mzungu*'s old office, now occupied by a local woman who would not hire Moalana. They were feeling too small, these days. Moalana could not discover what had happened to his parents, and he went back with the boys.

Eventually, by the time he was nineteen or so—he didn't know his age exactly—he was getting some boys of his own. And they were roaming around. There were hijackings, ambushes, shootings, *blood*. Moalana was good at it. All under the aegis of Hatashil. They were soldiers, Moalana explained to his boys, not criminals. "Very political" said Hatashil to his lieutenants, said the lieutenants to their Moalanas, said Moalana to his boys. Sometimes Hatashil distributed great wads of cash, and all were jubilant. Mostly Moalana and his boys were left on their own.

Live with Hatashil's dream in your hearts. Sometimes Hatashil was gone for a long time. Sometimes he or his lieutenants reminded them to shoot at NSF soldiers, or set up a roadblock. "Protect your land," was how they always put it. Most importantly, they periodically gave Moalana new Kalishnikovs, boxes of ammunitions, old fatigues. They gave him a durable Nokia cell phone. Years of these gifts and the language of war—"the armed struggle continues"—inspired Moalana. Eventually he was proud of Hatashil, almost as of a father, even though he'd only met him a few times. Thus Moalana's elation when Hatashil had invited him to sit under that gnarled acacia, just the two of them, and had given him a "special mission."

Moalana felt the old .38 in the pocket of his mesh shorts as he watched the waiter bring the goofy *mzungu* his Mirinda. He missed the shoulder holster. He had taken it from a man he had killed when he was fifteen. But it was too conspicuous.

53

Francisco was reading *Alice in Wonderland* to his daughter Maria when he heard the helicopter approach. The day had been so absolutely still and hot that the cicadas themselves had sounded desperate, on the verge of combustion. Francisco closed the book and left for the airstrip, leaving Maria confused but indifferent to Lewis Caroll's abrupt departure from her psyche. When her father was not reading to her, she could not remember what the story was about. Francisco read to her every day.

Francisco was not expecting anyone that day and never had unexpected guests. Helicopter arrivals were also rare. He recognized the chopper, though. He waited with his men on the edge of the green strip, feeling the hot mechanical air on his face.

Milton Lambert followed his passenger, Dale Lunt, out of the helicopter. Francisco had never liked either of them, and they had never before come together. He didn't judge them for their business, rather he had observed on their various visits their similar disregard for the ocean, their heavy footfalls, their indifference to the staff. But he greeted them warmly. Lunt did not express any apologies for arriving out of the blue. *Imperial* thought Francisco. They had become like praetors. *No doubt the Neros in Lunt's congress will set fire to their country soon enough,* he thought darkly. Lambert asked for a drink while they were still driving to the house.

"Hassan will take care of you," said Francisco as he deposited them on the big verandah. He called for Hassan, a short young man in glasses, and invited his new guests to dine with him that night before he left them to find his daughter. But he was too distracted to read to her anymore.

All afternoon Hassan stood quietly at attention on the verandah. He brought a stream of Tuskers and prawn sandwiches to Lambert and juices and gin and tonics to Lunt. As the sun went down the men left the verandah for a swim and a shower. Hassan went to Francisco's office to report. Francisco sat at his driftwood desk, looking out beyond his laptop at the Indian Ocean, which shone in the still heat. His mind had been wandering. He had often found himself thinking abstractly since that young man Teak had stopped the rape of his daughter. At first, Francisco had been vengeful. He had found the offending cook and beaten him in private, then put him on a leaky dhow to the mainland and warned him never to come back. But now, as Hassan came to his desk, Francisco was wondering what would happen to that cook after death. Francisco had thought about killing him.

"Well?" he said to Hassan. Hassan had been the best student at the schoolhouse Francisco had built on the island. Though young, he was observant, and nearly fluent in English. Francisco was very fond of Hassan and trusted him.

"They talked about the young man, Teak, who was here before," began Hassan. "The fat one, Lambert?"

"Lambert."

"He talked. He said he took Teak somewhere in his helicopter."

"Where?"

"Somewhere on the northern border, I'm not sure."

"That's all right, then what?"

"*Alafu,* Lunt was angry." Hassan paused. "It gave me a bad feeling for Teak."

After Hassan left him, Francisco considered Lunt's chances in the afterlife. Looking out at the sea, at its every wrinkle, he considered the possibility that each soul was permanently in transit and could shift cardinally on the strength of a breeze. *That was what these imperials didn't understand*.

He sat staring for several more minutes. His daughter wandered into view, dragging her feet through the small waves along the shore. She was helpless. Francisco was grateful to God that he lived in such a way that he could provide her freedom and safety and comfort. Away from institutions; here, where what existed truly were the interactions between men and women on the beach and not the inscrutable designs of ambitious businessmen and evangelicals. He was Catholic, and distrusted institutions.

She could be pregnant now, thought Francisco. *If it wasn't for that young man.* He looked through his rolodex, the older cards yellow and curling from a decade by the sea. Teak had left his Wildlife Fund card. Francisco looked from the card in his hand to his daughter on the beach and wondered how dangerous Lunt might actually be.

54

Teak caught the eye of the waiter and ordered another Mirinda as he calculated the chances of surviving a dive across the table. Slim, he decided. Toma could certainly kill him there in the daylight. So Teak took his eyes from Toma and watched a young man, about his own age, stroll by. Cutoff denims, barefoot, an open, faded yellow shirt, and the midday sweat glistening on his broad forehead. A flash drive, on a cord around the guy's neck, swayed with his stride. Teak wondered what was on the drive. *Fanta kid grown up.*

He felt irrationally that the answers to all his questions were on that drive. And then with a sudden, dropping clarity he considered what was rational—the gun on him across the table. It was logical. This was what he had signed up for. He hoped he didn't die at that table, and steeled himself. *I can beat this.*

"Stand up," said Toma quietly. Teak did. Toma walked behind him, hand in pocket, directing him across the dusty street to a shaded, narrow alley of concrete walls. It was very hot and as Teak reached for his handkerchief to mop his face

Toma hissed at him and he stopped. Teak was thinking slowly, pushing the thoughts of his death away, searching for a solution. At the moment when he faced the pitted wall and all his history compressed into a fearful void in his gut he said, "Wait." He remembered.

"You haven't been to the base at Brava, have you?" said Teak.

Toma had never known where Hatashil was from. *No one did.* No one had known him as a child, which was rare. His legend, of course, had been that of the orphan. Orphaned by his enemies. He had always come from somewhere else, which made sense, because he always had money. Toma had often wondered where the money came from. Politics was about family, cousins, tribes—they were what determined influence. But Hatashil had always been more of a loner, beholden only to his men. This was why, mirroring the NSF, these men—or boys—came from across the Horn. It was a larger kind of family. But none of them knew where his resources came from. Hatashil smiled and conspired and confided competing stories to different men. Toma saw this misinformation and had once pressed Hatashil about it. He told Toma only that the fewer people who knew him, really knew him, the better. Which made sense. But Toma felt a twinge of insecurity, a small insult when Hatashil had not revealed anything about his money. And six months ago, when Toma had first learned of the shipping container in Brava, Hatashil had told him only that it was part of a coastal operation that would be revealed later. Toma knew such an operation did not exist. At least, he thought he knew.

Moalana, peering over the edge of the rooftop, directly down, watched Toma steady his gun behind the *mzungu*'s head. Maybe his job would be done for him. That would be good luck.

"Hatashil is not who you think," said Teak, sensing movement of the pistol behind his ear.

"Who is he then?"

Slowly, Teak turned around. "I think Saudi," he said, noticing that Toma seemed to be chewing the inside of his cheek. "If we go to Brava, we'll find out."

Toma pushed the pistol into Teak's face, opened Teak's jacket, and took the SIG from his waistband. He said if Teak was wrong, and they found nothing in Brava, he would kill him there.

Moalana watched them walk out of the alley together and climbed down to follow. Now maybe he would have to kill them both. Luck always goes away.

55

Jane gripped the arm of her seat and looked out into the infinite blue. She turned the music up in her headphones and tried to let Cat Power distract her from the hum of the plane, from the close beige walls. She was glad to be in business class. She hated being afraid.

When the attacks of September 11, 2001 had occurred, Jane had felt nothing her gut. She was only a teenager, and thought about the towers' fall in a political way. She disliked the boosterism that rose from the Liberty Street ashes. She disliked theatrics and was vocally horrified by the manipulation of spectacle by the mayor of New York. She thought what she did partly because she was a liberal Beacon Hill girl and partly because she absolutely knew that the men in power were corrupt. Now, Jane liked to say, if ever she heard a classmate rail against them, that "they're more weak than evil." She had picked this up at her family dinner table after the truth came out about the Katrina relief effort in New Orleans.

But that day on the plane, flying to John F. Kennedy from Jomo Kenyatta by way of London's Heathrow, she became extremely conscious of the 9/11 attacks in a new way. She drank more red wine than usual and she thought about sudden explosions, a rushing descent to earth that would seem to go on forever. The fear gave way to anger as she looked at her father gently snoring across the aisle. He worked in a finance tower, and now many of the people she knew at Harvard were to begin their own careers in finance towers, too. They all could have been killed.

She had known this before, but now she was furious. She suddenly understood vengeance. Like wanting to chew on something, snap it between her teeth. For the first time, she wanted theatrics. How dare they? These cowardly Muslims who would murder her father, murder finals clubs boys, murder Sylvia, murder all her friends who would be sitting at computers in downtown skyscrapers in the coming years? She wanted these Muslims punished, she wanted them executed.

"More wine?" asked the stewardess.

Jane had never believed in capital punishment before. Thinking it over now, on the plane, she considered the possibility that Teak had changed her mind. Maybe she was trying to be as tough as he was. They had made plans to see each other back in Cambridge, and he had given her a mission. She had beat him to it, of course, suggested it before he could even get the words out. "Set the record straight," he told her. But she had told him first and she was determined. She would start at the *Crimson,* she decided, but the story could go national, she was sure. But it was also about Teak.

Saying good-bye at Kenyatta International had been difficult for her. She had wanted to say I love you but didn't. It was too soon. She had wanted to tell Teak that she had a boyfriend—*an African, actually*—and that she would leave him. But she didn't. She had wanted to secure everything in that moment as they said good-bye because she was certain Teak was *an ideal partner*. But she knew she could not secure anything, really. Even if she told him that she loved him and that she was leaving her boyfriend. He had seemed distant, as if, confirming her worst fears, he had gotten what he came for now that they had fucked on safari. She was sure that Teak had lots of girls.

But Jane was also sure she was important to him. She could recognize longing. She knew it especially from the times when men had kissed her and almost grimaced as they did because, she supposed, they wanted or needed her so badly. David was like that sometimes because he was lonely and poor and homesick. He had that grimace. And she had felt something like it in Teak, that morning everyone else had gone out looking for the leopard. But not quite. It wasn't physical and it wasn't needy—more empty, like the open door of a rocket ship, vacuuming her out into space. She didn't know what it was, she only hoped that it made him come back for her. Stay with her.

Teak would want those terrorists executed, Jane thought. Even though he was gentle. That was easy to fake, though, she knew. She faked it sometimes, too. The whole thing could have been a big fake-out. *Who wouldn't want to fuck me on safari for a week.*

Jane unbuckled her seat belt and went to the bathroom. She looked into her eyes in the mirror and was reminded of David. They had this joke about eyes. Early on she could tell that he was nervous, *or something,* about dating a white girl. So she had always made a point of how similar their eyes were.

Jane had dark eyes despite her fair hair, not as dark as David's but very dark.

She would be sorry to break up with him. *But you can't control where love takes you,* she thought, you have to follow it, have *faith*. The plane dropped suddenly and Jane was terrified. As she gripped the handle on the wall her new fear of terrorists returned. She fought with herself to dismiss the idea that the plane had been hijacked. When the turbulence stopped she returned to her seat and saw that her father was still snoring.

56

As they left the alley, Toma insisted they ride together in his old blue Peugeot.

"Long drive," Teak said. "My truck is better for the roads."

"Not up to you," said Toma, and then more diplomatically, "I love this car." They both knew the truth. Toma wanted to keep the gun on Teak and he felt more comfortable doing this in his own car. "You drive."

Toma played Motown on the tape deck as Teak drove them to the coast.

Neither spoke while the music played. When Toma had no more tapes the silence was uncomfortable and they drove on without looking at each other. The car bumped and jarred crazily over the bad road but Teak drove fast anyway.

And then Toma turned and looked at Teak and told him that maybe the problem was him. Toma talked very fast about the "old boys network" and how it had been boiled down to its greediest, most arrogant base. Teak's people didn't really respect the rest of the world.

"That Baggara herders have cell phones. Useful to you, no? *Fascinating*," Toma mocked him. "Everywhere you go, the truth runs away from you people. The question is simple." He was laughing now, chilling Teak. "What was the plan?"

Teak was quiet.

"I asked a question," said Toma.

"We keep working," Teak responded.

"The simple answer is betrayal," said Toma.

Toma turned the music on again and Sam Cooke sang scratchily over the cassette player and they drove without speaking. *Live at the Harlem Square Club, 1963.* After the album played through, Toma spoke again, his round-rimmed glasses flashing at Teak.

"This is my stadium," he said. "I'll play golf, football, whatever I want. If you try to play with me, I will kill you. I'll skin you alive or pay two of my guys to do it. Come to the immigration office at the border and I'll kill you there. Or go to the UN office and I'll drive there in a white official car and shoot you. One, two bullets. Or I'll have one of my guys do it." Toma took a breath. "You can't play with me here."

"I know," said Teak, but thought, *yes I can.*

Brava. A coastal town much like the one where they had first met, but bigger. A refugee town, surviving despite years of war. Goats nosed along the cracked road. The sun licked at the fishermen dragging their nets at the shore as small plastic bags and other garbage washed around their ankles. Here, too, a dilapidated boatyard. A pair of men caulked the hull of an ancient tugboat.

As they drove along the sea Toma pointed to a particular stack of shipping containers, old, unmoved in years. There was a camera attached to the corner of a blue container at the bottom of the stack. The camera was trained on a bolted door.

"We'll need tools," said Teak, "and darkness."

The afternoon cooled and gray cumulus clouds rolled low across the horizon. Seabirds wheeled and fought over the garbage at the shore. Waiting, Teak and Toma sat and drank warm orange Mirinda at a café across from the yard where the pair of laborers worked on the hull of the tugboat. Teak watched them work. Toma watched Teak. At sunset the laborers knocked off work and put their tools on carts and rolled the carts to a garage in the corner of the boatyard.

"Come on," Teak said, rising.

"What are you doing?"

"Going to fix the car. Give me the keys."

Toma hesitated. Teak looked at him impatiently.

"Kill me if I'm wrong. You have the guns."

Toma tossed him the keys. Teak drove the car around the corner and pointed it down a small hill toward the boatyard. Then he popped the hood and reached in and pulled a wire off the coil. He put the wire back in place but didn't quite set the connection. Toma gave a short confused shout and brought his hands to his head. Teak sat behind the wheel and turned the engine over. It sounded like it would start on the next turn but didn't.

"Easy to fix, if you know where to look," he said as he got out. Then he opened the trunk. "Roll it down in neutral. Right into the garage." He tossed the keys back to Toma. "Tell them they can fix it in the morning." He looked around to make sure no was watching and climbed into the trunk. "I'll call you when it's time to meet at the container." He silenced his phone and closed the trunk over his head.

"Send lawyers, guns, and money," Toma muttered to himself as he released the brake. He put the car in neutral and rolled down into the garage. The foreman was surprised when Toma told him he was staying at the hotel up the way and they could fix it in the morning.

The trunk smelled of motor oil and something sweet that Teak could not identify. He groped along the edges of the darkness until he touched some organic smoothness. In the blue light of his phone he saw a pile of date pits. Teak rubbed a pit between thumb and forefinger. He was good at waiting, and the skill had been valuable to him. The trick to it was to think. So in airports, in his apartment as weeks went by waiting for a contact to reemerge from the bush, as he waited endless minutes for the daily necessities of life in Nairobi, Teak had thought. When he had first articulated this trick to himself, watching the Green sisters bicker in a first-class lounge at JFK as they all waited to fly to Kenya that first time, he wondered why anyone ever minded waiting. There was so much to think about. What was six hours in an airport when his mind could go anywhere? But then he discovered the problem—he always thought about the same things. He tried to think about locations, academics, politics—ideas. But no matter his concentration, the ideas passed and he thought about the people he knew, and ultimately himself, often his ambitions as an agent—*to be decent, do good work*. And then the trick became accepting the doubt that came with those ambitions. *What the fuck am I doing?* That doubt returned to him there in the trunk. He pushed the thought away, accepting the wait. Staying alert. *What the fuck?*

Teak listened carefully for sounds outside the trunk. He had not heard anything after his first hour in the garage. He waited another two, listening closely. Hearing no sound he called Toma, let the phone ring once, and hung up. Then he brought his hand up to the trunk handle where he had wedged his handkerchief into the catch mechanism. He pulled the handkerchief to open the latch, but the latch was stuck. Teak pulled again, and tried to work his fingers in, but the door wouldn't open.

He twisted his body, pulled his folding knife from his pocket and quietly sawed through the cardboard paneling behind the backseat. He broke out a section of the panel and then cut through the cushion until he could force his shoulders through the old foam and squeeze himself through. He climbed over the front seat, found the keys on the floor, got out, opened the trunk, and retrieved his handkerchief.

The garage was dark but he could see the few, old tools neatly shelved along the walls, parts arranged in boxes on workbenches, scrap in a corner pile. He found what he was looking for quickly. The blowtorch was not light but Teak hefted it easily and climbed out through one of the high back windows. He had memorized the layout from the garage to the shipping container when he had driven by earlier. There was a fence with concertina wire around the boatyard. The only exit was past the little guard hut at the gate. After that it was a right turn out, a right turn back to the water, and a short walk along the piers to the first stack of containers and good cover.

Flattening himself against the side of the garage, Teak looked around the corner to the hut at the gate. A young guard in a faded Intersec cap sat reading a Bible under a buzzing fluorescent light. Leaning against the wall by his feet was a pump-action shotgun.

Teak moved quickly but quietly up behind the guard, who didn't notice his presence until the final moment. As the guard turned around Teak knocked him in the temple with the blowtorch tank. The Bible fell closed next to the shotgun.

The moon floated brightly. Toma waited in the shadow of Hatashil's container. When Teak stepped from between the two nearest containers Toma immediately had the gun on him. Seeing it was Teak, Toma exhaled and lowered the gun, but only a little.

Teak took a perforated black silencer from his pocket and offered it to Toma.

"Do you want to shoot the camera or shall I?"

Toma took the silencer and twisted it onto the SIG. With a *clack* his shot shattered the lens and they heard the tinkle of glass falling to the ground. As they moved to the door Teak put on his sunglasses and ignited the blowtorch. Toma stood guard. Teak cut through the bolt quickly and the door slid open on smooth, silent rollers.

Inside, in the dark, the metal of the container was warm to the touch from the day's heat and the air was still and oppressive. Teak turned his penlight on the wall by the door, illuminating a switch. He slid the door closed to prevent any light from leaking out into the night and flipped the switch.

With a hum of a waking electric generator, fluorescent lights flickered on the ceiling and conventional lights in simple sconces came on along the walls. The container was now very bright. Along one wall ran a long table set up as an office: two laptops, a scanner, a printer, and a fax machine. A tall filing cabinet stood in one corner. At the far wall was a king-sized bed and a nightstand. On the nightstand were magazines, books, a glass, and an empty pitcher. The *Economist,* but no Koran, Teak noticed.

On the opposite wall was a large locker, which Toma opened as Teak booted each of the computers. Inside, he found an RPG-7 launcher and three rockets, a pair of assault rifles, and a string of hand grenades.

In the filing cabinet, Teak found what he was looking for. From a manila folder he took out a Saudi passport, several Western health insurance cards, and several bank and credit cards. *An emergency exit,* thought Teak. The name was identical on all of the documents. It was not Hatashil. It was Emudi.

"He's the son of the chief of Saudi Intelligence," said Teak, laying the documents down one by one, thinking of Alan Green. "Stole a lot of money from his father's friends."

Toma faced Teak in front of the long table, the documents spread between them. He opened his mouth and then closed it. This could not be. He had to know what the American knew. Quietly he said, "so the Saudis told your people to kill him?" He tightened his grip the handle of the gun as he looked at Teak.

"We wouldn't kill him," said Teak. *But I don't know that.*

Toma remembered when he had first met Hatashil, his surprise at how Hatashil spoke Arabic. Like a Gulf Arab. Proper, textbook Arabic. I studied diligently, was all Hatashil had said about it.

"One phone call from Bandar . . . ," said Toma, studying Teak's face. He loosened his grip on the pistol. "Give me a cigarette please. Fuck."

Toma took a cigarette from Teak and walked to the door. He thought of the lies he had told for Hatashil, each one in the service of . . . what? He could have left, gone to live in London or Cambridge. Susan Lowell had offered him that, but he had lied to her consistently and held to his lies. He had not left. He had stayed and fought for Hatashil. He had never wanted to leave, become an immigrant. But now.

"This doesn't change anything," said Teak. "He's still the best man."

Toma didn't hear him. He had opened the door to step out and smoke his cigarette. Teak heard two shots and saw Toma's legs trip over the threshold, his body falling out of view. The container seemed to vibrate. Teak ran to the door and as he saw Toma lying there, the side of his face gaping with a bullet wound, he collided with Moalana, who was rushing him with his pistol. Moalana realized he had made a mistake. He had been nervous and hoped that they would walk out together. But only one had walked out.

Teak grabbed Moalana's pistol, wrested it from him and drove the barrel into his nose. He heard a crack and Moalana bellowed and kicked out. Teak shot him in the leg and then knocked him unconscious with the pistol.

Through the door Teak saw a truck coming toward the container. He didn't want to leave Toma's body but there was no time. He was kneeling to close Toma's eyes when another bullet ricocheted off the container past his head. The shot had not come from the truck. He ducked back in. He stuffed Hatashil's identity documents in the pocket of his jacket. Checking quickly out the door he saw a dozen irregular soldiers approaching the container, moving from cover to cover. *Hatashil's people*.

Teak ran to the locker in the back of the room and retrieved one of the rocket grenades and the launcher. He poked his head out the door, drawing a sustained burst of fire, and ducked back inside. After a single breath, he stepped back out the door, fired the RPG into the ground just ahead of the advancing irregulars, and ran past the next row of containers as they were blinded by the fireball.

The truck had turned toward him and two men fired from it, leaning out the windows. Lights were turning on all along the waterfront. He darted into a dark space between two containers. He caught his breath again and sprinted around the rear container to arrive behind the truck. Teak took careful aim and shot the driver through the rear window, then bolted forward and shot the two passengers as they turned around. As the truck stalled, he pulled the driver from behind the wheel and got in, turning the ignition and putting the truck back in gear.

He drove out of town with the two dead bodies still in the back seat; one looked Ethiopian, one Somali. *Weird alliances. New tribes*. Miraculously, the gas tank was full. *No such thing as luck*. And then Teak remembered the CNN footage of the U.S. pilots being dragged through the streets of Mogadishu. When he was ten minutes out he dumped the bodies.

Driving south through the dark, he unsilenced his phone and considered calling Lunt. He had a theory. It was probably the Sauds who had tried to kill Hatashil. They'd wanted to for years and they'd finally found him.

The phone beeped in his hand. There was a message. It was Francisco. He told Teak that Lunt and Lambert had been on Funzi and that they had been talking about him. "It gave me a bad feeling," Francisco said. "I am just calling to tell you that."

Teak tossed the phone on the passenger seat and decided that though he did not know exactly what was happening, he did know not to trust Lunt and that, in fact, he had never liked him. And if Lunt was tight with Lambert, he was sloppy. Green had never spoken highly of him anyway. *I have my own agents,* Teak thought, *and I report to a higher authority. Me.*

He drove through the night and the next day, straight to the airport. On the tarmac at Kenyatta he called his boss at the Fund and told him that he had a family emergency. He had to return to the States.

57

When Jane returned to campus the weather had turned cold. It called for the late fall clothing she liked best. She wanted to look good when she broke up with David but she felt guilty and small for wanting that.

Equivocating as she unpacked her bags, she worried that perhaps her affair with Michael Teak had been nothing more than that, or perhaps a fever dream such as she had been warned of on her way to the malarial zone. But she had not gotten malaria, and she had spent those days with Teak. And then he had called her, given her a list of assignments. First, he told her to torpedo anymore bad press about Professor Lowell at the *Crimson*. Second, go talk with Lowell about researching Hatashil. But not to mention him. "Open a dialogue." It seemed so much more serious than anything she had ever done. Her teeth almost chattered when she got off the phone. Jane told herself not to lose her sense of irony, even though Teak sounded so convincing, the matter so serious. But then she thought about the sound of Teak's voice as she called David and told him to meet her at Daedalus.

They kissed a brief hello at the bar and David ordered tequila shots for them. He didn't know why he did it, exactly. He was feeling extremely uncertain of himself.

"Tequila," said Jane, "what's up with you?"

"A lot," said David.

They drank the shots and left Daedalus. As they walked through the dead leaves on Mount Auburn Street Jane told him about the Masai Mara—he'd never been. Jane could see in David's face how much he wanted her and she felt worse every minute she was with him. The closer she was to him physically the harder it would be to break up with him. She almost didn't want to. When he put his arm around her shoulders she again allowed herself the possibility of staying with him, if only not to leave him standing in front of her dorm. But then she thought of Teak and was fortified and told David that they needed to stop seeing each other.

"Why?" David asked.

"It's just time." She couldn't make herself tell him about Teak, though she felt she should.

David didn't know what to say, so he said, "I'm giving a speech tomorrow. You'll like it. It's all about how Hatashil killed my cousins."

"That was your village?"

David shoved his hands down into his pockets and looked at the ground. He slowly kicked a pile of skeletal leaves out of the gutter. She wrapped her arms around him but he did not hug her back.

"I'm so sorry. But you can't make that speech." There was desperation in her voice he'd never heard before. "It doesn't matter about you and me. But it's all wrong."

"It doesn't matter?"

"I was wrong. Lowell was right. Hatashil didn't do it."

"How could you know that when everybody else knows the opposite?"

"I don't mean *we* didn't matter. But I was just over there and—"

"Were you, on your *safari*?" David had never been acid with her before, and he enjoyed it.

"Just don't give the speech. Please, for me."

"You just dumped me."

The next day, David opened his speech staring at Alan Green in the audience. "My name is David Ayan," he said, "and Hatashil killed my family." Green nodded back at him in approval.

58

Of all the bad news Susan Lowell had gotten in the preceding weeks, none injured her as much as the speech she watched David give. Everything seemed completely fucked up. He said that it was easy to forget how complicated problems are when you live inside the ivory tower. Susan wished she could have helped him edit the clichés out of his speech, even as he insulted her research.

She went to dinner with Razi that night, glad that they were good enough friends that she could be down around him. She couldn't do that with Harry anymore. Especially recently, since he had been asking her if she was all right all the time. And they hadn't been able to fuck right.

She and Razi met at the Central Kitchen, which was candlelit and warm. A frost covered the windows looking out on Massachusetts Avenue. The menu was expensive burgers and Cobb salads and so on and there was a long wine list. Razi was happy he had finally gotten her to come out for some drinks, away from what he saw as her perfect family for a night.

Razi and Susan were among the last people there. They had been talking work all evening, more guessing about what had happened between Hatashil and the United States. Susan always had good theories, thought Razi. He had been drinking since the afternoon but he didn't think she had noticed when she arrived. He didn't care now anyway.

"I heard Marina's out on bail," Susan said. She felt like she had been faking the whole conversation. "Maybe we'll all meet up again."

"Not safe," said Razi.

"Maybe Toma would work something out for me." *This is what I am supposed to do. I am supposed to go back out.*

"You can't even get him on the phone. And the reason you can't go back is the work you've already done there." Razi couldn't make himself clear. "The Pulitzer."

"I'm sick of this fucking prize," said Susan. "And that's so cynical of you."

"What's cynical? You want to leave your family," he said, "go back into that mess?"

"I thought we never talked about *the risks,*" she made a mock frightened face at him. "Just trying to do good work."

"What about the kids?"

Susan almost laughed. "You sound like they're yours."

"They should have been."

He had not meant to say that. Susan froze, coffee cup between saucer and mouth. He had said it seriously and it seemed to hang in the air with a kind of malice.

"And you should leave Harry for me," Razi continued. "I love you. *There's* a reason not to go back."

He realized as he was saying this that he was making a

mistake but he was drunk and did not, perhaps could not, stop himself.

"Sober up, Razi," was what Susan said, putting down her cup.

"You knew all along," he told her.

"That you're a drunk? Yes, Razi." She stood to leave, but he grabbed her hand. She took it back. "I'm not going to do this," she said, and walked out of the Central Kitchen into the frigid Cambridge air.

After a few moments Razi paid the check and walked outside, too. He looked for Susan but she was gone. He smoked a cigarette. And then, as the first tiny snowflakes of the winter began to fall around him on Massachusetts Avenue, he smoked another.

59

In the business-class cabin of the 747 flying from Heathrow and JFK, Teak was struck by the light blue eyes of the stewardess pouring him coffee. He had seen few people, lately, who had those eyes. It was the first lesson in so many of the courses at Harvard: most of the world population resides in the southern hemisphere and they don't look like you. The pale freaks of the north are the minority. Some woman on the long walk north, post Pangea, had stopped on her path and squatted and given birth to a freak. Maybe they had beaten the strange-eyed child to death with pieces of bone and rocks. Maybe they worshipped it. But somewhere along that very long path one of the freaks survived. And the stewardess was descended from that freak and so was Teak. It was not the short story of trade and immigration, it was the long story of geography. And while the people he was going home to, his people, were concerned with the short history—whose parents had been holocausted, the subtle play between Muslim fathers and hip-hop sons, the great Indian diaspora—somehow the longer story wasn't as important to them.

That was the problem. Or so it seemed to Teak, right then. *I am confused by the details. I have to step back.* Hatashil was an enemy of the Saudi royals. *When we found out,* Teak thought, *of course we stopped supporting him.* And Lunt went a step further, tried to kill him. *For his career*. Teak imagined how it played out in Lunt's head. The Hatashil mess was too close to the Sauds, the NSC, the White House. Naturally anyone with career aspirations would have stayed well away from the file. But Lunt couldn't, it got dumped on him. So he tried to blow it up. *Short stories and shorter stories*. Teak was sure Atwater would know something about Blackford, and Blackford had Delta written all over him, maybe Joint Special Operations. And when Teak figured that connection out, he would take it all to Green.

He resisted the temptation to take Hatashil's various passports out of his carry-on just to look at them again.

The familiarity of a yellow cab from JFK into Manhattan was as refreshing, in its way, as diving into the ocean after a long time in the desert. As Teak watched the enlarging skyline he dialed Atwater, hoping that he'd be in New York for the holiday. It was nearly Christmas. Atwater answered and Teak was happily surprised. "I could use a drink right now," Atwater told him.

They met at a back table in the Cedar Tavern, just south of Union Square. It was a place they had gone in college and they couldn't think of any place else. Neither of them lived in New York anymore. But Teak was happy with the location. The old wood and the yellow lighting and the passably attractive waitress seemed to put Atwater at ease, perhaps as it had the abstract expressionists many years before. The place was really just about drinking.

"So, how long are you in New York?" Teak asked.

"My dad had a heart attack."

Teak was sorry about that and as Atwater explained that it wasn't all that serious and that his father was already home, Teak also realized that neither Charlie Atwater, nor probably the abstract expressionists, were actually at ease in this place. *Really just about drinking*.

"I've been out of school for a long time," said Atwater, "but every time I come home to New York for Christmas I feel like I've got exams hanging over my head, you know?"

"Winter break," said Teak. Atwater had put on some weight. Teak doubted he could do a backflip anymore.

Teak did not bring up Blackford until he was ordering Atwater his fourth Dewar's. "Seemed like a stand-up guy," said Teak. "I met him in Nairobi."

"Yeah, Blackford," said Charlie Atwater wistfully, sipping at his scotch.

"So, is it long term policy stuff you're working?" asked Teak.

"I could be designing the Iraqi seventh grade curriculum if I wanted. Truth is," Atwater leaned in and whispered, "you can really pull some funny stuff if you get a little team together."

Teak waited.

"Now, of course, it's not like a prank. But what if? *What if*, right? What if we could change something for the better, or just see if we could?"

"Who's we?"

"It's Thursday night. Guys like me, you know the staffers who come up with the ideas. And that's really it. You get into these weird jobs, and who's in on it with you? Who are your friends? The people you drink with on Thursday night is who." Atwater tapped his glass on the table for emphasis.

"I wonder who Director Harrison is drinking with on Thursday night," said Teak.

"Spare me the conspiracy theory. We're already in. Can't give it to *China*. It's just trade, you know, econ ten."

Charlie was drunk now. Teak smiled. "You never studied, did you Charlie?"

This cracked Charlie up. He laughed and laughed.

"You know all that special forces stuff I did?" he said, leaning in again. Teak could see Charlie showing off. He never lost that vanity, thought Teak. *Still doing backflips*.

"Really just between you and me," Atwater said.

Teak waited again.

"Blackford is an alias for a Delta guy. Guy's still in, but works out of this Joint Ops shop. Real thing, no patches on the uniform. That's what I was."

"No shit," said Teak. "And he's still Delta?"

"Delta's long-lost son at Joint Ops."

Teak moved right on after that. Back to Charlie himself, school, friends, women. But there it was. It had been the Americans, or at least American led. *Lunt. Green*. Teak kept a straight face. But the brick in his stomach was not from surprise. *You*. It felt as though he had known all along. *You delivered the cell phone.*

Outside, Teak put Atwater in a cab and watched it pull away into the light snow, bound for Park Avenue, where the trees were dressed in white light.

Teak flipped the collar of his tan jacket up against the snow and walked to his parents' empty apartment on Gramercy Park.

They always spent December in Sun Valley now. In the kitchen he drank a bottle of water and then went to bed and tried to fall asleep quickly. He wanted to be fresh on the first shuttle to Washington National in the morning, but did not sleep all night.

60

By midnight everyone would know. That was what the punches were told. David was unable to concentrate on his studies. The books on the desk before him lay open but unread. David checked the clock on his phone again. The whole day had been a wait. He had jumped when someone brushed by him at lunch, thinking it might be a signal. He tried to resign himself to not getting in but kept calculating his odds. About eighty-twenty—damn Robert—he figured at first. As his mood changed over the course of the day, so did the spread.

At a quarter to twelve his phone rang.

"David Ayan?"

"Yes," he said. His voice stuck. He had to clear his throat and repeat himself. As he did so he was talking over the caller's voice but he heard the directions anyway, which were simply to go outside.

Out in the courtyard underneath a tree dedicated to John Winthrop, there were thirty or so young men in suits and overcoats. They stood, exhaling a line of white clouds in the freezing air. It was beginning to snow and the small flakes collected on their shoulders. David didn't know what to do. But then the young man at the head of the line smiled at him. He was the sleepy club member from the bus, and he looked sleepy now, but he was smiling. "Welcome to the club, Mr. Ayan," he said, and extended his hand. David shook it. The next member said and did precisely the same, and David went down the whole line. They were all wearing leather gloves.

After David shook the last one's hand they all turned and walked away in a line.

I did the right thing, thought David. He silently thanked Green. When he learned, the following year, that Green had nothing to do with the final selection of a member—that it was all up to the current undergraduate members—he would still be thankful to Green, vaguely, loyally. As he would be for a long time. At the moment, though, David was only ecstatic. He grinned across the snow-dusted Quad, let loose a small whoop of victory.

"You know," said the sleepy member to another as they left the Quad, "I really like being stoned while we do this. They all just radiate, you know? So happy."

"Yeah," the other member said. "We gotta get some more weed for back at the club. You guys going to Daedalus first?"

61

Razi sat alone at a table in the Cellar. He drank willfully and quickly. He didn't want to talk to anybody at the bar but was glad the bar wasn't empty. If it had just been him, the bartender might have tried to chat. Force him out of his own head.

Razi felt as though he had just sat down when last call came. Then Lucas and Willy sauntered into the bar in their tuxedoes. Willy carried a large black umbrella. They decried a coming blizzard and asked for one last drink as they had made it just in time. The bartender allowed this, and Lucas and Willy both ordered margaritas. The bartender changed his mind so they settled for gin and tonics.

Soon Razi, Lucas, and Willy were the only people left in the bar, so Lucas and Willy sat down with Razi. He looked at them without speaking. Their constant banter was somehow soothing and he nodded sure, he'd go on with them for further revelry. *The brotherhood of barflies.* He knew that he didn't want to go home to sleep, only to wake the next day and face the hangover and what he knew he had done.

The three of them set out at a slow walk for the *Lampoon* Castle. In a room concealed behind a bookcase they smoked a spliff, their ashtray made of a rhino's foot, and Lucas and Willy each did a couple of lines. Razi was only reacting by then, but he was happy to be along for the ride. *Like a carnival ride,* he thought, *or a roller coaster,* he could simply hang on and it would take him around and up and down and he could postpone sleep and his reckoning with the dawn.

Willy and Lucas wanted to keep moving, so they set out walking again. They were having some great laughs at the zombie they had brought along for the ride and he didn't even seem to care. It was a slow night, but Lucas and Willy didn't mind as long as they stayed lubricated, agile.

Razi looked at the snow as they walked. The first light of day was glowing and the sky looked like dark, smoky glass and the flakes still fell through the yellow streetlight. The three of them paused at one of the security phones. Above each such phone on campus was a blue light. These blues lights, freshmen were told during orientation, were what to run to if they felt threatened, if they thought they were going to be raped or robbed. The snow was particularly beautiful, white-blue, suspended in air, as it caught the light from these security-phone markers. No one ever talked about using these phones, thought Razi, just how pretty the lights were. He had heard that mentioned.

Lucas and Willy decided they were hungry.

"I've got just the ticket, old sport," said Lucas to Willy. Then to Razi, "are you familiar with Zipcar? I actually have the key right here. Shall we to our chariot?"

"To the International House of Pancakes!" concurred Willy.

When Razi sat down in the front seat of the same red Mini Cooper that they had driven before, Willy was annoyed, but Razi would not move. Fuck if he'd sit in that little backseat, Razi thought through his fog. He leaned his head against the window as they drove through the silent snowy streets. He dozed off.

The crash came just over the Charles River. Lucas was too drunk to regain control when the Mini Cooper began to skid across the on-ramp to the Pike and he was not a very good driver anyway. Razi woke up in that last instant. All the old reactions pumped through his veins from a hundred different fuckups and bad scenes all over the world. He was only alert for a moment, but it was enough to see the semi coming. The semi skidded over the icy slush as it tried to brake, but when it hit the Mini Cooper it rolled and crushed the small red car.

62

The morning that he arrived in D.C., Teak and Alan Green walked along the edge of the reflecting pool. The sky was slightly darker than the marble of the Lincoln Memorial and the air was still and very cold. Teak told Green what he had discovered about Hatashil and about the paramilitaries and even what had happened to Toma. Green looked straight ahead as Teak spoke.

When Teak finished he asked Green if the operation at the village was American. They were at the far end of the pool looking out over the reflected sky.

"No," Green sighed, "we don't know who they were."

They looked straight at each other for the first time that day. Green was old, thought Teak, his face deeply lined, his eyes very tired. Alan's phone rang.

"Hello, sweetheart," Green said. He listened, then, "see you at seven." He hung up and said to Teak, "Dinner with the girls."

"I know about Gary Blackford," said Teak. "I know it was an American operation. And you do, too."

Green looked over his shoulder at the Washington Monument and then back at Teak. Teak almost felt sorry for him. His godfather didn't seem to know what to say.

"I never wanted you in any danger," Green said. "The truth is, I didn't know in the beginning."

Green sounded as though he was talking about the weather. He said the Pentagon had found out who Hatashil was first and that when Joint Ops heard they took the file from defense and Langley. These days they had their own Delta teams. Lunt hadn't known either, at the beginning. Green said, "I'm sorry you had to be the last man to know."

"And you don't care that we betrayed him?"

"You're too close. No one is ever more than an agent."

"We tried to kill him."

"Don't be a child. Please," Green put a strong hand on Teak's shoulder and squeezed so hard it was almost like a threat. "There is no reason," he said, "to expose yourself."

"This is not right," said Teak.

Green shrugged and turned to leave. "I know," he said. "I just let you see."

"No," Teak reached for Green's arm.

Green turned back to him. The wind gusted and cradled what Teak said next, and Green saw it in his face before he heard it, a twisted, ugly look he had never seen on Teak before. Green forced a laugh. "You don't understand," he said, "the Sauds were furious. "

"Fuck you," said Teak.

So young, thought Green. He turned away again and walked toward the Washington Monument and Teak saw the stoop in his shoulders. He briefly imagined chasing Green down and hurling him into the pool, watching him splash and struggle and the ripples coursing and distorting the reflection. Instead, he took several deep breaths and stood at the pool looking down at the reflected sky, untroubled but for the wind. Then he caught a cab back to the airport.

63

Director Harrison got Green on the phone and started the conversation with congratulations for getting one of Susan Lowell's advisees to come forward at the Action Conference and talk about how Hatashil had attacked not just one of Hatashil's own villages but one where this particular student had relatives. He saw it on Fox News. Brilliant. Then he asked what happened with Teak.

Green sat in the window of a chain coffee shop. He hadn't wanted to answer Harrison's call but he had. Lately their relationship had been terse. Harrison had accused him of getting caught up in what didn't matter.

"He's off it, removed himself," said Green.

"What did he say?" Harrison had called from the bathroom of his office in the White House, where he had been rubbing at one of his liver spots as he examined it in the mirror.

"Nothing really," said Green.

"What did he say?" Harrison snapped, issuing an order this time.

Green hesitated. Harrison waited.

"'Fuck you.'" Even though they were not his words, he enjoyed saying them to Harrison.

"Theatrical," said Harrison. "And you didn't think this aggression was important?"

"He won't be a problem."

Harrison disagreed. He thought Teak was a liability, had already identified himself as a problematic officer by disobeying orders. He also knew that Green had stopped Lunt from surveilling, perhaps incarcerating, Teak.

Alan Green tried to reassure him about Teak not being a problem but Harrison cut him off. "Why don't you get back up to school, Alan. Maybe you can find a new *boy*."

Harrison hung up. He was pleased. He had been losing confidence in Green for a while now and wanted to let him know. The next call he made was to put Teak under surveillance. He was a liability, could expose too much.

Light jazz played in the coffee shop where Alan Green stared down into the now cold blackness of his coffee.

At his desk the next morning, on the other side of the world, Lunt read a restricted e-mail about looking into Teak's time in Africa and putting him under surveillance. He went outside for a celebratory cigarette, to the back corner of the compound in the shade of a large bougainvillea. *Knew it from the moment I met the kid.*

Back inside at his desk, he was surprised to find a message for him from Director Harrison. Calling back, he bounced his foot on the floor. On hold for five minutes, Lunt suddenly and with great clarity saw an opportunity. An impressive idea for the director, who, for whatever reason, had made this file a personal project.

"Are you familiar with a woman named Marina Levy?" Lunt began.

64

Susan Lowell's ringing BlackBerry woke her at dawn. She hoped it was not Razi. Rolling over to the night table she saw the drifted snow out her window, pink in the dawn light.

The number was blocked. "Hello?"

"Dr. Lowell," said a voice she did not recognize.

"Who's calling?"

"I'm a friend of Toma Ali Mugabo. It's important that we meet as soon as possible. Please be at your office within the hour. Thank you."

"Hey," Susan began. She didn't like being railroaded. *Insulted, accused, humiliated in the national press, yes, but railroaded on the phone, not me. Ha.* "What's going . . ." but the connection was severed.

Susan looked up and down deserted Cambridge Street as she approached the high glass doors of the Knafel building. Inside, it was quiet and her steps echoed in the lobby. The door to her office was closed but unlocked. She always locked it when she left. She was unnerved, but opened the door without hesitation.

Teak stood at the map next to her desk, backlit by the morning sun through the window. She recognized him immediately. He had aged—his face had a rougher texture than she recalled, and the very beginning of lines triangled out from the corners of his eyes. He tapped the one yellow thumbtack in the map with his forefinger.

"I'm sorry to have come into your office like this." He moved to the front of her desk.

She was struck by his calm. He had broken into her office but he seemed so clear-eyed and purposeful that Susan offered him a seat. She knew that look in his eyes. *I used to have it*. She sat down at her desk and began to shuffle papers but stopped when he told her that her friend Toma was dead. Susan's heart fell and what came into her mind was Toma singing some lyric as he drove her and Razi along the coast.

From inside his jacket Teak produced a folder and placed it on her desk. Susan opened it: the passport and credit cards Teak had taken from the shipping container, and a photograph captioned "Gary Blackford." Susan Lowell inhaled sharply as she opened the passport.

"Why do you have a thumbtack in that village on the map?" Teak asked.

"I have a student from there," she said.

"Joint Special Operations command took it out."

Lowell's heart fell again, for David. She thought about how he had named each of his cousins in his speech.

Teak continued, "And they'll try to take out Hatashil again unless they're given a very good reason. A better reason then the Sauds." He nodded at the folder on the desk and said, "Gary Blackford is the alias of the Delta commander of the operation."

"Who are you working for?"

Teak ignored the question. "No one's been returning your phone calls," he said. "There's misinformation circulating, and you don't know how it's happening, right?"

"I, well," she struggled and then relented. "Right."

"Now you can write the story, professor. I'm your first source."

"You'll go to jail."

"It's important to me that Hatashil know Toma did not betray him. *We* did. Toma only helped me to understand that."

"Toma and Hatashil knew each other?" said Susan. *Of course.*

Teak stood up. "E-mail me your questions. Clear it up. Clear your name. There's an address inside," he said, pointing at the folder on her desk.

"I'm not going to just do this. Why should I even believe you?"

"I bet this belongs to your student," Teak said, taking the Harvard mug from the village out of the side pocket of his coat. He put it down hard on the desk. "Maybe you could give it back to him." Teak walked out the door.

Susan Lowell put her hand to her head and then, out of habit, as she was thinking, checked her e-mail. One new message. It was from Bill Bester, that friend of Razi's who worked out of D.C. The subject heading read "Razi." Susan opened it.

65

Robert sat in a café on Brattle Street called Algiers. This was his favorite café because he liked the music they played. He read the paper. The picture on page one was of Willy and Lucas shaking hands with each other in front of Professor Susan Lowell at the party celebrating her Pulitzer Prize. The editors had disagreed about running the picture. Some believed it was in bad taste because Lucas and Willy seemed to be clowning. Lust for life, countered others. The chairman of the photography board had pointed out that it was the most recent picture they had. He didn't see why they were wasting time arguing about it. And anyway, there were plenty of pictures of the tuxedo guys. They trouble was finding a picture of the other guy, the Nieman Fellow. Were they just going to use the stupid headshot or what? Weren't there shots of him with rebels in the Congo and shit like that?

Robert turned the page. A much shorter story concerned the charges being brought against a sophomore after allegations of assault at an off-campus finals club event. *Fock.*

There was also, Robert noted with some surprise, a photograph of David at some kind of Africa group news conference. Robert read with horror that a number of David's family had been killed in something called Hatashil's massacre. His rage came back and he didn't know what to do. He just knew he wanted to get away.

The music changed and Billie Holliday came over the speakers. He didn't know her story exactly. She had been a prostitute or something, he thought, and then had made it big. He liked the idea, identified with the underdog. The song they were playing was one of his favorites. *Love me or leave me or let me be lonely* . . . At the bridge the piano switched from jazz to a classical riff, Mozartean. Robert had always liked that switch. It was another thing he had tried to explain to his parents that they hadn't understood. If he were expelled, he'd have to go back to them, at least for a little while. And it didn't look good. His smarmy senior tutor advocate had told him as much. Spencer was a seventh generation legacy. *Seven fockin' generations.*

But Robert had a plan. He reached into his backpack where it lay on the floor by his feet. It was full of economics course work, but he had printed something different out the night before and brought it with him. The transfer application to Juilliard was not easy but it started with an essay question and Robert knew what he wanted to say. His first line was simple. *I am a pianist.*

66

There are many kinds of grief. E-mail is a new medium but death is a very old one, perhaps the oldest. That is, if death is a medium at all—a means, a channel, an avenue. It may be that death communicates nothing, that it is merely another phase of disintegration, another pose for the ashes and dust on their return from two feet to space. But if death does communicate something, like Razi occasionally thought, that news might be the most valuable news we could ever get. Because it would be universal news, and yet configured specifically and perfectly enough to stop the heart of every man, woman, and child in a different way.

Susan Lowell got the news about Razi in her office. For the first time in her life she had no desire at all to work. She went home and sat on her roof and wept.

67

By that afternoon the sun had melted much of the snow and the day was too hot for a heavy coat. For the first time since his return, Teak was not cold in his tan jacket. He waited for Jane on a bench by the Charles River, where he used to run, reading the *Crimson* in the bright sunlight reflected off the melting snow. In that day's story about Lowell, the paper explained that a student and advisee of hers, David Ayan, had condemned Hatashil for killing his cousins.

He saw Jane walking toward him from a long way off. As she got closer he could see a few strands of her hair blowing from under a fedora. He had told her that he would see her when he was next in Cambridge and so he was keeping his word. He had come to see Susan Lowell, not to see Jane, but he wasn't going to tell her that.

Before Teak said hello, Jane said, "isn't this weather strange?" Her heart beat hard and fast enough for her to be aware of it and she smiled at him, her face flushed. "I wish I knew how to fix this planet." She took the paper from his hand, looking at the Lowell-Ayan story.

"I tried to stop that one," she said, "but Krazmeyer, he's the editor, he's—"

"Listen," said Teak, "I have to go back to Washington today."

Jane got it from his tone right then, and stared out over the river as he continued on. He explained that he had to clear some things up with the Wildlife Fund. The job wasn't good anymore, he told her, and he needed some time away to clear his head. It was a lame story, he knew, but it was almost true. He told her he was going to travel for a while. Not work, just travel. He would stay in touch as best he could but she shouldn't wait for him.

It was a few moments before she looked at his face again, and then she felt ill. Teak was sorry that he wouldn't know Jane better. But not as sorry as she was. She wanted to work something out. "I mean, when are you leaving?"

"The three fifty train."

You should always just do what you want, Jane thought fiercely. *What was the point if you couldn't do what you wanted?*

"When are you coming back?" she asked.

"I don't know," said Teak.

Jane looked from his face to the newspaper again, the picture of David giving his speech.

"I tried," she said, pointing. "I tried to make him believe that Hatashil was innocent." Jane could not believe it, but she was starting to cry.

"That doesn't matter," said Teak. "But it was good of you."

Actual tears from behind her eyes, rolling out into the warm winter weather. She never cried. But she found she couldn't stop, and her ideas about chemical mysteries all fell down her cheeks.

"But you are coming back," she said. "Right? And we can get together then?"

"I don't know," answered Teak, honestly.

68

There were flowers in Susan Lowell's office again. No piles of roses this time, only a small mixed bouquet in a blue vase. She supposed her assistant had put it there. Everyone knew how close she had been to Razi. There was a card. The bouquet was from Henry Rose, head of the history department, with condolences. It surprised her.

She sat down and looked at the bouquet. The proper names of the flowers escaped her. She was certain she knew, but it was as if that specific knowledge had been erased from her memory. She looked closely at the leaves. The veins and stalks in perfect evolutionary, mathematical alignment. She thought about Razi and about luck. She had come to the office to try and work, but couldn't concentrate. She reread the open document on her laptop, the only thing she had written that day. *The American intelligence community first supported Hatashil and then betrayed him, and is now covering up that betrayal. Hatashil is, in fact, the estranged and ambitious son of Saudi Intelligence Director Al-Emudi. The responsible elements within the intelligence community did not at first realize this. I know this because I made the same mistake.*

There was a knock at her door. Susan was silent. The knock came again.

"Come in," she said.

David walked in.

"I must drop your seminar," he said. "And I am here to do it in person. "

"I'm so sorry about your cousins," said Lowell. "Please sit."

David did not sit. He thought about telling her that he had not expected his talk at the conference to be played the way it had been. The *Crimson* had called it "shocking." But he was too angry at her.

"They say you killed someone for Hatashil," he told her.

Susan Lowell shook her head and almost laughed. David suddenly saw how fucked up she was. She had dark circles under her eyes, her famous sunglasses were just barely keeping her hair in place. No makeup. She looked sick, he thought. He still did not sit.

"It's too late to drop," she told him. "Nearly the end of term. I'll have to fail you. Please, David, sit."

David finally sat, though he did not disguise his reluctance.

"Hatashil didn't attack that village." She pointed at the map on the wall with the yellow tack in it.

"How do you know?" said David, raising his voice. Then he said, "I came here because it was the right thing to do. "

She could see the recent loss pulsing in him and her empathy was sharpened by her own grief over Razi. "Are you all right?" she asked

"*Safi.*" He told her. *Clean.* They had never spoken Swahili, but he knew she spoke it.

"I know because . . ."

David interrupted her. "I don't want to talk about this right now." He unconsciously reached a hand out to the bouquet on her desk, touching his fingers to the vase. "Can I go, please. You can just fail me, I guess."

"You don't want to know?" she asked.

"It's not my life, professor."

There was a pause. Susan tried something else.

"Do you have plans for this summer? Going home?" She regretted the second question as soon as she asked it.

"No." David paused. Then he said, "I applied for some internships."

"What sort of internships?"

David listed the banks and consulting firms where he had applied.

"I didn't know you were interested in that kind of work."

"I just started to be. I want a good money job."

"You know, maybe I can help you get an internship. My husband is a partner at Dillon Wilcox, here in Boston. Why don't you send me your CV and I'll give it to him?"

Another pause before David asked his question. "Will you get me the job?"

Susan paused for a moment, thinking. "Yes, David. I will. But you won't get the job if there's an F on your transcript. So you can't drop the course now."

"Then I'll see you in class" he said, and left.

Susan turned in her chair and looked out the window at the Science Center and Annenberg. The snow was melting. The freshmen were lined up outside for lunch. Several were having a snowball fight. She looked down to the bottom drawer of her desk where she had locked the mug and the Hatashil documents. She put the documents on her desk and looked at them. She turned the mug over in her hands, took a deep breath, and realized that she wanted to go back to work more than she had ever wanted anything in her life.

69

Paris, France, 200X

That morning a young American named Michael Teak sat at an unvarnished wooden table in a new restaurant and read a newspaper editorial about his government, which was at that time the most powerful in the world. The story was in French and said that his country had been at war for twenty-five years, in one part of the world or another. This was true. He had never known a time of peace, though he had never thought of it that way until this moment.

A week after his confrontation with Susan Lowell, when Charlie Atwater had called him and asked if he knew about this Harvard professor woman who was leaving messages at his office in Washington, Teak had quit his job. He had arrived in Paris for the end of the winter and begun running again. He ran all over the city, up the steep roads of Montmarte, along the white gravel paths of the Luxembourg Gardens, around the Place de la Bastille. Though he followed the news, he did not work, or think about work. He lived in the small hotel he always stayed in when he was in Paris. An original map of the city from 1739 hung on a wall of the lobby. Sometimes he had a coffee in the courtyard bistro, where flowers were just beginning to bloom.

Now that the spring had come he was thinking about what to do next. Not knowing, he figured, suggested graduate school. He wrote drafts of applications to schools of international relations, to law schools; he was even considering postbaccalaureate programs that would lead to medical school.

The waitress came by with his coffee and sandwich, blocking the light through the windows and the view of the young neighborhood residents strolling outside, along Rue de Pearl. A little boy in a fancy tweed playsuit glided by on Rollerblades, shoulder-length blond hair tied back in a ponytail. Teak was thinking of the Fanta kid less frequently, and when he did, the thought passed through his mind, like wind through the front door and out the back of an open, empty house.

After his sandwich he walked south toward the Seine, brown and constant. As he crossed over he wished that Jane was with him. He had come to Paris for a kind of vacation, with a notion of starting everything over, but now that he was here, walking up to the Musée Rodin behind a couple of American kids in denim jackets, that wasn't how he felt. Instead of going into the museum he walked to his nearby hotel. Oddly, there was no one behind the little desk, so Teak got his key off the hook himself. He stopped for a moment in front of the city map, planning where he might run the next day. Then he walked up the three dim flights to his room. He dropped the key on the night table, tossed his khaki jacket over the desk chair, and lay down on top of the white cover. Sleepy after lunch and his walk, he napped.

The bathroom door opened slowly. Marina Levy moved quietly to the edge of the bed. She was conflicted about what she was going to do. She was sure she was being used to ends she did not understand, and she did not like that. But a good relationship with those people in Washington was so valuable, and this was the biggest, and best paying, kind of favor. The one that no one asked for.

Acknowledgments

For various combinations of shelter, trips, and editing, I am indebted to the Korschens and Van Aardts in Lamu; Liban Ali Mugabo in Kigali; Olivia de Dieuleveult in Paris; Ed Lintz in Williamsburg; Dave Evans and Fleur Jearvis-Reade in London; the Bickertons in Seminyak; Hugh Malone in Maine; the Wilcoxes; Peter Matthiessen; Will Hearst; Alex de Waal; my agents Eric Simonoff and Bob Bookman; and my publisher Morgan Entrekin. And for a home in between, to Joanie and Terry and Stacey McDonell.